Jake felt a warm body beside him.

It had been years—eleven, to be exact—but Caley Lambert was exactly as he'd remembered her. His gaze drifted down to her lips, soft and full and slightly parted. She was all woman now—sexy, soft and warm. And she was sleeping in his bed....

Jake leaned over, touching his lips to hers. She obviously wanted something to happen. It was a pretty bold move...but Caley had never been known to wait when she wanted something. And he could only hope she wanted him as much as he was starting to want her....

"Jake," she whispered.

The sound of his name on her lips was like fuel on a fire. His desire surged and he kissed her again, deeper, harder this time. This was Caley, the girl he'd wanted all his life. She could be his now....

But as he settled above her, an uneasy feeling came over him. Something wasn't right.

"Caley. Open your eyes."

Her lashes fluttered, and a moment later she was looking at him, first in confusion, then in absolute shock.

He'd known it was too good to last....

Blaze™

Dear Reader,

I've always had a soft spot for stories about childhood sweethearts. And when I was working on this idea for THE WRONG BED series, I thought about twisting that concept a little and giving you a hero and heroine who weren't quite sweethearts but still managed to carry a pretty big torch for each other.

Jake and Caley come back to the small lake community where they'd spent their summers to serve as best man and maid of honor at a Valentine's Day wedding between their two siblings. The book is set in my home state of Wisconsin. And since Wisconsin can be pretty cold in February, I had to find new ways to keep my hero and heroine warm—and then hot. But I have to admit, it was a pain dealing with all those layers of clothes.

As you're reading this, I'm sure February is delivering its usually icy cold weather and bitter winds here in Wisconsin. I hope *Your Bed or Mine?* keeps you nice and warm wherever you are.

Happy reading,

Kate Hoffmann

KATE HOFFMANN
Your Bed or Mine?

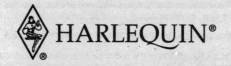

TORONTO • NEW YORK • LONDON
AMSTERDAM • PARIS • SYDNEY • HAMBURG
STOCKHOLM • ATHENS • TOKYO • MILAN • MADRID
PRAGUE • WARSAW • BUDAPEST • AUCKLAND

ISBN-13: 978-0-373-79383-9
ISBN-10:   0-373-79383-9

YOUR BED OR MINE?

www.eHarlequin.com

Printed in U.S.A.

ABOUT THE AUTHOR

Kate Hoffmann has been writing stories for Harlequin Books since 1993. Her first book, *Indecent Exposure*, told the story of a tabloid reporter and a tabloid photographer after the same salacious story. Nothing much has changed in fourteen years, except the color of Kate's hair. She's written over fifty books for Harlequin, including twelve in the popular MIGHTY QUINNS series. Kate lives in a small town in Wisconsin with her cats and her computer. Besides writing, she works with high-school students in theater and musical activities. She also enjoys golf, movies, music of all kinds and genealogy research.

Books by Kate Hoffman

HARLEQUIN BLAZE
234-SINFULLY SWEET
  "Simply Scrumptious"
279-THE MIGHTY QUINNS:
  MARCUS
285-THE MIGHTY QUINNS:
  IAN
291-THE MIGHTY QUINNS:
  DECLAN
340- DOING IRELAND!
356-FOR LUST OR MONEY

HARLEQUIN SINGLE TITLES (The Quinns)
REUNITED
THE PROMISE
THE LEGACY

HARLEQUIN TEMPTATION
847—THE MIGHTY QUINNS:
  CONOR
851—THE MIGHTY QUINNS:
  DYLAN
855—THE MIGHTY QUINNS:
  BRENDAN
933—THE MIGHTY QUINNS:
  LIAM
937—THE MIGHTY QUINNS:
  BRIAN
941—THE MIGHTY QUINNS:
  SEAN
963—LEGALLY MINE
988—HOT & BOTHERED
1017—WARM & WILLING

1

HUGE SNOWFLAKES drifted down through the night sky, spattering against the windshield of Caley Lambert's rental car. She watched through tired eyes as the wipers slapped them away, the rhythmic sound lulling her toward complete exhaustion. Her eyelids fluttered and she felt herself drifting, then reached down and opened the window.

The chilly night air was a slap to the face and Caley drew a deep breath. The flight from New York had been late getting into Chicago and by the time she'd arrived, the airport hotel had given away her room. Left with nowhere to sleep, she'd decided to drive the two hours to her parents' lake house rather than waste time searching for a room.

It wasn't so much an urge to get home that sent her into the midst of a snowstorm, but the fact that Caley just hated wasting time. After eleven years of living in Manhattan and seven years of working the cutthroat world of public relations, she'd learned to be very efficient with every minute of her day. She didn't waste time on anything that couldn't get her ahead in the world professionally. She worked out because the gym was a good place to network. She belonged to seven different professional organizations because all those names looked good on her résumé. And she had worked sixteen-hour days for seven years because that was the way to get herself a partnership.

"So what am I doing in North Lake, Wisconsin?" she muttered.

Her younger sister, Emma, had called a few weeks ago, insisting that Caley come home for the week before Valentine's Day. Emma had a very special event planned at the lake house, but she refused to give any details, only that every one of the Lamberts should be in attendance. Caley's parents had been married on Valentine's Day thirty years ago, so it hadn't been difficult to guess at the purpose of her sister's plans.

An electronic version of Mozart's "Eine Kleine Nachtmusik" interrupted Caley's thoughts and she glanced over at her cell phone sitting on the passenger seat. Snatching it up, she looked at the caller ID, then tossed it back onto the seat. Brian. He'd called at least twenty times since she'd left New York for a business trip in San Francisco a few days ago. So far she'd avoided answering.

She and Brian had been exclusive for nearly two years and he'd planned to come to North Lake with her and meet the family. But at the last minute, he'd canceled, begging off because of work commitments. It was at that moment Caley realized her relationship with Brian had become a waste of time. Between out-of-town business trips and busy schedules, they'd spent three nights together in the past month—not much considering they lived in the same apartment.

She squinted through the snow, searching for the sign pointing to West Shore Road. There was a time when she'd known every inch of the tiny town of North Lake. She'd spent every summer of her life here until she'd gone to college.

Even after years of being away from this place, and in the midst of a chilly winter night, she felt a familiar sense of excitement course through her. She remembered the frantic packing the day after school let out for the summer. And then came the ride from Chicago to the lake in an overstuffed minivan, her mother behind the wheel. Her older brother, Evan, always sat in the front and controlled the radio while Caley sat between her younger siblings Emma and Adam. The youngest, Teddy, was wedged into the far back seat between the suitcases and the boxes of kitchen supplies. Her younger siblings had always worn their swimming suits on the ride up so they could jump out of the car and into the lake without having to change.

But Caley had always had other things on her mind. With each mile that passed, she'd grown more excited, the anticipation building, the nerves fraying. What would he look like? Would he be exactly as she remembered or would he have changed? Had she changed? Would he see her differently? Would this summer finally be the summer when she'd kiss him?

Year after year, drive after drive, her every thought had always been focused on him. Even now, Caley found herself falling back into old habits. Jake Burton. He'd been her fairy-tale prince, her knight in shining armor, her schoolgirl crush and her first love, all wrapped up into one incredibly hot boy.

His family had the summerhouse next door. They'd all summered together for years: the five Lamberts and the five Burtons, an unruly tribe of kids known around North Lake as the Burtberts. For years she'd looked at Jake like her older brother, Evan—an icky, gross, burping and spitting cad who had more cooties than she cared to count.

Then, one day they were swimming out to the raft and Jake dunked her under. She'd gone under as an eleven-year-old girl and surfaced a teenager with her first crush. He'd been thirteen that summer and a handsome boy. Even now she recalled his pale blue eyes and his perfect teeth. How little droplets of water had clung to his dark eyelashes as he smiled at her and how his face was so smooth and tanned she felt compelled to reach out and touch his cheek.

When she had, Jake had slapped her hand away, a confused frown wrinkling his forehead. But from that moment on, she'd been in love. It was only later that her hormones had turned chaste puppy love to teenage lust. And later still to feelings that bordered on obsession and finally, ended in humiliation.

She drew in a deep breath and sighed. Over the past eleven years, she'd managed to visit the lake house only when Jake was certain to be elsewhere. Yet, with each visit she'd secretly hoped that maybe she'd run into him again, maybe she'd have a chance to undo the mess she'd made the night of her eighteenth birthday.

Her phone rang again and Caley cursed as she picked it up. But this time, she didn't recognize the number, only the Manhattan area code. Now that she'd been named a partner, her boss was free to call her at any time, day or night, and John Walters had taken advantage of that fact more than once. Caley wondered what kind of emergency had come up at nearly 4:00 a.m. Manhattan time.

She flipped open the phone and held it to her ear. "Hello?"

"I figured you were screening so I was forced to call from the payphone on the corner."

Caley recognized Brian's voice and bit back another curse. "I really don't want to talk to you. I said everything I needed to say before I left. It's over."

"Caley, we can work this out. You can't just end it. Everything was going so well."

She laughed, shaking her head at his ability to spin the situation. Brian was one of the most successful young lawyers on Wall Street. Like her, he could put a positive spin on the worst disaster imaginable.

"How can you say that?" she asked. "We barely see each other. And when we do, we have nothing to say. We talk about work."

"What do you want? I can talk about other things."

"That's not the point," Caley said, growing more frustrated. Usually, she was able to express her views clearly and unemotionally. But this time she had no idea what she wanted. She just knew she didn't want to come home to Brian anymore. For a long time, her life had felt out of balance and this was the only way she could think to fix it.

"What *is* the point?" he asked.

"I—" she took a deep breath "—I'm not happy."

"When has that ever made a difference to you? You work nonstop, you never take a vacation, every minute of your life is planned. Of course you're not happy. Who would be? But, Caley, that's the way you like it."

"Not anymore," she said. "It just doesn't feel

right." Suddenly, she felt a panic grip her body. Was this the right thing to do? Was she really ready to give up? A buzzing in her ears made her dizzy and for a moment she thought she might pass out. "I—I have to go. I'll call you when I get back and we'll sort out all the details. Goodbye, Brian."

Caley quickly pulled over to the curb and rolled the window down, breathing deeply of the cold night air. For the past month, she'd been fighting these panic attacks. They'd become an almost-daily occurrence. She'd blamed them on the stress of being named a partner, on living in Manhattan, on her doubts about Brian. But Caley sensed that none of these factors were really the cause.

The sound of a siren startled her and Caley looked in the rearview mirror to find a police car pulling up behind her, lights flashing. She hadn't even been close to the speed limit! But when she'd pulled over to the curb, she might have swerved too suddenly in the snow. Caley watched in the side mirror as the police officer got out of his SUV and approached the car. A sudden shiver of fear raced through her. She'd seen the stories on the news. Rapists and serial killers posing as policemen. Caley brushed the thought aside. This was North Lake. Things like that happened in New York, not in Wisconsin.

When the officer reached her car, he tapped at the window with his flashlight. Caley pressed the button on the console and the window slid down an inch. "Show me your badge," she demanded. He held it out and Caley snatched it from him. It looked real enough. She opened the window a little more and handed it back.

"License and registration, please," he said.

"I-I'm not sure I have a registration," Caley said. "This is a rental." She pulled her license out of her wallet and handed it to him, then reached for the glove box. "The car comes from Speedy Rental at O'Hare. I have the rental agreement right here." She handed him the paperwork, then peered out at him. "I wasn't speeding."

"You were talking on a cell phone," he replied. "We have an ordinance against that in North Lake. Have you been drinking, ma'am?"

"No," Caley said, stunned by his question. "I just pulled over because I was tired. I needed some fresh air."

He paused as he examined her license. "Caroline Lenore Lambert," he muttered. "You're Caley Lambert?" He shone the flashlight in her face and Caley squinted.

"Yes."

"One of the Burtbert kids?"

"Yes," she replied.

He turned the flashlight off, then leaned down, sending her a friendly smile. "Well, don't you remember me?" He pointed to the name tag pinned to his jacket. "Jeff Winslow. We went out on a few dates the summer of...well, it doesn't really matter. I took you sailing. I ran the boat aground over near Raspberry Island and you called me an idiot and dumped a can of Coke on my head."

Caley did remember. It was the sailing equivalent of running out of gas on a deserted country road. She also remembered how Jeff Winslow had tried to kiss her and feel her up and how he'd chided her for acting like a priss. Most of the boys she'd dated that summer before college had served just one purpose for Caley—they were a feeble attempt to make Jake Burton jealous.

"Of course," Caley replied. "Jeff Winslow. My goodness, you're a policeman now? That's almost ironic considering all the trouble you used to cause."

"Yeah. A misspent youth. But I've reformed. I got a degree in criminal justice, then worked for the Chicago P.D.," he said. "Then I heard they were looking for a police chief here and I thought, what the hell. I'd been shot at four times in Chicago and figured my number was coming up. So I came home." He chuckled. "I guess you've caught yourself a lucky break."

"I have?"

He flipped his ticket book closed and tucked it back into his jacket. "I'm going to let you off with a warning." He returned her driver's license. "As long as you promise not to talk on your cell phone while you're driving. It's against the law in the entire county and it's a pretty big fine."

"Thank you," Caley said.

"So, what have you been up to? The last time I saw you in North Lake you were just out of high school."

"I work in New York," Caley said. "I don't get back much."

"Too bad," Jeff said. "Living in the city is great, but I never really appreciated this place until I left. There's something special about North Lake...something peaceful." He shrugged, then tapped her window with his finger. "You drive carefully, Caley. The roads are slick. And if I catch you talking on your cell phone again, I'm going to have to give you a ticket."

"I understand," Caley said.

"Good night, then."

For a moment, she sensed he might have something else to say. But then, he turned and walked back to his SUV. A few seconds later, the lights stopped flashing and Caley took that as her cue to pull out onto the street. Moments later, she spotted West Shore Road and made the turn, Officer Jeff following her at a distance.

The houses along the shore were dark, most of them unoccupied in the winter, and she squinted to see the mailboxes through the snow. She passed by the sign for the Burtons' driveway; the next one belonged to her parents' house. A small light glowed at the end of the drive and she turned in and steered the car down the steep slope through the leafless trees, holding her breath the entire way. The SUV continued past, Officer Jeff apparently satisfied that she'd made it to her destination.

She switched off the ignition and stared at the house through the icy car window. It was even more picturesque in the winter, the roof covered with snow, icicles hanging from the gutters on the white clapboard facade. Looking at the peaceful setting, Caley knew it would be impossible to get any work done while home with her family. And though she felt she needed a break from work, she knew she couldn't. So she had made a reservation, starting the next night, at the inn downtown. Between Evan's three kids and the usual craziness that occurred when her boisterous family was together, Caley was certain she'd need a place to hide out.

Caley stepped out of the car and grabbed her bags from the back seat. She couldn't help but glance over at the Burtons' house. There was a light on in the kitchen, but the rest of the house was dark. No doubt Ellis and Fran Burton would be at the anniversary celebration. But there would be no reason for their children to be invited. Still, Caley had to wonder if there was a chance she'd see Jake. And if she did, what would it be like between them. Would he remember that night on the beach? Would he pretend as if nothing had happened?

It had been eleven years. Maybe it was time to let it go, Caley mused. She'd been a kid with a crush. She hadn't seen Jake since the night before she left for NYU. Until now, the memory of that night had always brought a surge of regret and utter humiliation.

They were adults now and if he wanted to rehash her silly teenage indiscretion, then she would simply refuse to discuss it. Certainly he'd made mistakes in his youth that he didn't want brought up around his family. Caley tried to think of one or two just in case she needed ammunition.

They had gotten into all sorts of trouble as kids. Even now, Caley was amazed that she'd managed to avoid a life as a juvenile delinquent. But she and Jake had been a pair and she'd been the only one of the Burtberts who ever accepted his dares.

She smiled. Once, they'd caught a squirrel in a live trap and let it go inside the police chief's cruiser. Then there had been the time she and Jake had stolen a bike from the town bully. The next morning, the kid found his bike bobbing up and down on the raft just off the public beach. That trick had gained them a lot of admirers, although they never admitted to it. And then, there had been all those times they'd broken into their "fortress," a deserted summerhouse on the east shore.

The house was dark and silent as she slipped inside. No one ever locked the door when the family was at home. She stood in the spacious foyer and took a deep breath, the familiar scent teasing at her nose—a mix of the lake and leaves, old wood and furniture polish and the vanilla candles her mother loved to burn to take the damp out of the air. Once, she'd known every inch of this house, every secret hiding place, every sun-drenched window. It had been her very own castle.

Caley slowly climbed the stairs then walked down the hall to her bedroom. But when she pushed the door open, she saw the room was already occupied—Evan's kids, two in the bed and the youngest in a portable crib.

She carefully closed the door and walked across the hall. Emma would probably have room in her bed. She slipped inside her sister's room and closed the door behind her. Caley set her bag down and walked to the bed. The room was chilly and Emma had found a down comforter and was buried beneath it, her pillow pulled over her head.

"Em?" Caley whispered as she stood over the bed. She shrugged out of her jacket and kicked off her shoes. Emma had always been a heavy sleeper. Caley sat on the edge of the bed. She could probably find an empty couch downstairs, but she was too exhausted to search. She'd catch a few hours' sleep and check into the inn for a long nap in the morning.

Caley slipped out of her jeans and crawled beneath the comforter, pulling it up to her chin. She closed her eyes, her mind drifting back to the last summer she'd spent at the lake house. Jake had been home from college that summer after his sophomore year. From the moment he'd arrived, Caley had been completely and thoroughly obsessed with him. He was gorgeous, lean and tanned and so incredibly sexy that Caley was sure she would die if she couldn't be with him.

The summer had passed, Caley trying anything and everything to get him to notice her. Finally, on the night of her eighteenth birthday party, she had decided to make a bold move. College was just a few days away and she didn't want to leave for NYU a virgin. So she'd screwed up her courage, gotten Jake alone on the beach, torn off her shirt and asked him to make a woman out of her.

Caley groaned inwardly, pulling the comforter up to her nose. Even after all these years, the thought of her stupid offer was enough to bring a blush to her cheeks. She closed her eyes and said a silent prayer that Jake wouldn't show up in North Lake until she was gone.

He was probably miles away, Caley mused. Maybe even sleeping beside another woman. She frowned at the tiny sliver of jealousy that pricked at her thoughts. The torch she'd carried for Jake had been extinguished a long time ago. It wasn't jealousy. Closer to envy, Caley thought, for she had imagined Jake happy and settled and maybe even in love.

He probably had everything in life he'd ever wanted. And she was still trying to figure out what she needed to make herself happy. Caley thought she'd have all the answers by the time she was thirty. Now, her twenty-ninth birthday was just a few months away. There wasn't much time left.

Maybe a week away from New York and the life she'd built there would give her some perspective, a quiet moment to figure things out. Caley yawned, threw her arm over her eyes. She'd have plenty of time to think about all this tomorrow. Right now, she needed sleep.

THE SOUND OF A CELL PHONE ringing dragged Jake Burton out of a deep and comfortable sleep. He groaned softly, then realized that the electronic jingle didn't belong to his phone. It was only then that Jake felt the warm body beside him.

At first he thought he was dreaming, but the weight of her leg thrown across his thighs was real, as was the citrusy scent of her hair. He tried to move his arm and found her head nestled against his shoulder.

A name, he thought to himself. He was in bed with a woman and he couldn't remember her name.

Though he'd indulged in a number of one-night stands in the past, he'd pretty much given that up as of late.

The phone continued to ring and then stopped suddenly. Where had they met? Where had he been last night? Jake waited for the signs of a raging hangover to seep into his consciousness, but strangely enough, he knew he hadn't been drinking. If that was the case, then why couldn't he remember the woman?

"Think," he whispered as he slowly opened his eyes. His surroundings were completely unfamiliar. But then, slowly, he realized where he was. The Lamberts' lake house. Emma's bedroom. But if that was where he was, then who the hell was in bed with him? Surely not his future sister-in-law!

He pushed up on his elbow and squinted at the clock. Six a.m. He looked down at his bedmate, then carefully brushed the wavy dark hair away from her face. "Oh, shit," he muttered, snatching his hand away. It had been years—eleven, to be exact—but there was no mistaking that beautiful profile, the upturned nose with the light dusting of freckles, the flawless skin and the long lashes.

She was exactly as he'd remembered her, only Caley Lambert was no longer a gawky teenage girl. She was a woman. His gaze drifted down to her lips, soft and full and slightly parted. A very sexy, soft, warm woman. But what the hell was she doing in his bed?

Jake fought the urge to bend closer and touch her

face. God, he remembered those urges. Funny how they all came back so quickly. Just how many times had he thought about kissing Caley Lambert over the course of his life? A hundred, maybe two hundred?

The summer she'd turned eighteen it was all he could do to keep his hands off of her, from the moment he'd arrived at the lake house until the moment he'd left. He'd deliberately avoided her, just so he wouldn't have to think about it.

And now he had the chance. Why not take it? Why not see what he'd been missing all these years? He smoothed her hair away from her face and leaned over, then touched his lips to hers. As he drew back, she stirred and her eyes fluttered. A sigh slipped from her lips and she smiled.

Jake watched her warily. She obviously wanted something to happen between them or she wouldn't have crawled into bed with him. It was a pretty bold move, considering her parents were sleeping just down the hall. But Caley had been known for her bold moves and she obviously had become bolder since he'd last seen her. She lived in Manhattan. Hell, he'd seen *Sex and the City*. He knew what single women in New York were like.

"Do you want me to kiss you again?" he whispered.

"Umm." She snuggled closer, resting her hand on his bare chest.

"Umm" could be construed as a negative reply, but Jake decided that, coupled with her sleepy smile, it indicated a positive response.

He stretched out beside her, furrowing his hands through her hair and gently covering her lips with his. She seemed to melt into him, her body pressing against his as another sigh slipped from her throat. In his youth, kissing Caley had been an obsession and now that it was a reality, Jake was stunned by the sensations that coursed through his body.

It was just a kiss! But it was as if all of the pent-up desire from his teenage years had suddenly been released. And now, he could actually imagine what might happen between them.

His reaction to the kiss was immediate and intense. It had been a while since he'd had a woman. During the past year, he'd found himself searching for something that had been difficult to find—a woman who was strong and independent and not afraid to be herself. He was through with women who were willing to remake themselves into whatever they thought he wanted.

Jake smiled. He'd known Caley for years and what you saw with her was what you got. Even now, he imagined that she was just as stubborn and opinionated and determined as she'd been as a kid. God, he'd always admired her. She was the only girl he'd ever met who challenged him.

Her hand moved down his back, her palm warm against his skin, then slipped beneath the waistband of his boxers. He held his breath as she moved her fingers forward, to his hip. Though he hadn't woken up to a morning erection, he'd managed to remedy that situation in quick order by kissing her.

He pulled her beneath him, his fingers still tangled in her hair and molding her mouth to his. Her hips rubbed against his, his shaft hot and hard between them. There was something so exciting about touching her, something almost forbidden.

"Jake," she whispered.

The sound of his name on her lips was like fuel on a fire. His desire surged and his kiss deepened, his tongue plunging into her mouth hungrily.

This was Caley, the girl he'd known all his life, the girl he'd so carefully avoided. But she could be his, here in this bed. There was nothing to stop them. In the past, the time had never seemed right, but now, every instinct in his body screamed that the time was perfect.

As he kissed her, he found himself caught up in a fantasy that he'd lived a thousand times in his dreams. He slipped his hand beneath her T-shirt and gently cupped her breast, rubbing his thumb across her nipple through the silky fabric of her bra.

She shuddered, then arched against him, but still

her eyes were closed. An uneasy feeling came over him and for a moment, he thought she might be asleep and dreaming. Jake drew back and stared down at her face, watching her as he continued to caress her breast. "Caley?"

"Jake?" she murmured.

"Open your eyes."

Her lashes fluttered. She looked at him, at first with a blank stare and then with growing confusion.

"Morning," he murmured.

Caley frowned and rubbed her eyes with her fists. A cry of alarm slipped from her lips and then, in a rush, she pushed away from him, tumbling backward onto the floor, her bare legs tangling in the comforter. "Wh-what are you doing in my bed?"

"I think the more appropriate question would be, what are you doing in *my* bed?"

"Not your bed. This is Emma's room. It's her bed." She blinked, rubbing the sleep from her eyes. "And you're not her."

"Emma's staying at the inn in town so she can have a little peace and quiet. Our house was full, so your mother offered me the last empty bed."

Her phone rang again and Caley looked around the room, then crawled across the floor to retrieve her purse. She watched him warily as she flipped open the phone. "Hello?"

Jake grinned at her, letting his gaze take in her

long, naked legs and the lacy black panties. Yes, the gangly teenager was gone, replaced by a long-limbed, incredibly sexy woman.

"Yes, John. I understand. No, I'll get right on it. You'll have it by the end of the day. All right. You, too. Goodbye." She closed the phone.

"Boyfriend?"

"Boss," she murmured. "You were in this bed last night. With me?"

Jake nodded. Oh, hell, she had been asleep. "Yes. But I wasn't with you. Not in the biblical sense. We were just next to each other. And then, well, then you woke up." The last thing he needed was Caley to go running downstairs, accusing him of being a pervert. "Hey, it was an honest mistake. It was dark. I looked like your sister. How could you have known?"

A frown wrinkled her forehead. "Then we weren't just… I wasn't… Nothing happened, right?"

Jake winced. "Well, there was a little something, but that was an honest mistake, as well. I just kind of assumed you'd crawled in bed with me for a reason, so—"

She touched her lips. "You kissed me?"

"But you kissed me back. And there was some local-ized touching going on, but only through the clothes. Except you did put your hand down my boxers."

Her phone rang again. Caley opened her mouth

and snapped it shut, then looked at the caller ID. This time, she decided not to answer. Instead, she grabbed the corner of the comforter and pulled it off the bed to cover herself, leaving him in nothing but those boxers. She watched him warily, waiting for him to make the next move.

"Did you think I was someone else?" he asked.

"Yes," she snapped. But from the guilty look on her face, he could tell she was lying.

"Some other guy named Jake?"

"Yes. I happen to know three or four other Jakes."

He grabbed a corner of the comforter and pulled it over his lap. It would be hard to sell the "nothing happened" story with a raging hard-on pressing against the front of his boxers. Jake cleared his throat and forced a smile. "So, how have you been? It's been a while. How long? Eleven years?"

She nodded, clutching the comforter to her chest. Her cheeks were flushed and her breath was coming in quick gasps. And her hair, thick and wavy, was tumbled about her shoulders. She'd never looked more beautiful. Jake's gaze drifted down, stopping at the perfectly painted toes peeking out from under the blanket. She'd always had really pretty feet. He'd spent a lot of time looking at her feet when he was younger, simply to avoid looking at her breasts, which were also pretty incredible.

"Your mother said you wouldn't be arriving until this morning," he commented.

"I decided to drive directly from the airport. When did you get in?"

"Yesterday," he said. "So, what have you been up to?"

"Not much," she replied. "Just working. I'm still with that public relations firm that I joined right out of college. I was made partner last month. What about you?"

"I have my own design firm now. I'm doing mostly residential architecture. I kind of specialize in vacation homes based on classic camp designs."

"Interesting." She drew in a sharp breath, impatient with the idle chitchat. "What are you doing home? Why would you want to come to my parents' anniversary party?"

A slow realization dawned. Emma hadn't told her what was going on. Jake wondered if he ought to be the one to break the happy news or if she should hear it over the breakfast table. For now, it might prove a distraction from what had just happened. "This isn't an anniversary party," Jake said. "It's Emma and Sam."

She frowned at the mention of Jake's youngest brother. "Emma and Sam?"

"They're getting married."

At first she gasped, then regarded him with disbelief. This was the Caley he remembered. She always found a way to disagree with him, even if he was only claiming the sun rose in the east and set in the west. "Not funny."

"It's the truth," Jake said. "That's why we're all here. It's going to be a small wedding at the Episcopal Church in town on Valentine's evening. She's got the dress and they've got the license."

"They aren't even dating," Caley said.

"I guess they have been. They've been secretly seeing each other for the past three summers. They didn't want anyone to know. You know how our mothers are and how they've dreamed about making a match between the Lamberts and the Burtons. They got engaged on New Year's and decided to get married right away, before Fran and Jean could plan a big event."

"But they're only twenty-one," Caley said. "That's too young. What do they know about marriage?" She drew a ragged breath and stared at him, as if she were taking a moment to digest the news. Then, her eyes slowly dropped, first to his chest and then his legs. She pulled the comforter up beneath her chin. "Do you think maybe you could get dressed and—"

The door to the bedroom swung open and Caley's youngest brother, Teddy, stuck his head inside. "Hey, Jake. Are you going to want some—" His words died in his throat as he took in the scene in front of him. "Hey, Caley. You're home." He glanced over at Jake, then forced a smile. "Yeah, okay. Breakfast," he murmured as he closed the door.

"Oh, no," Caley moaned, scrambling to her feet. "No, no, no. Now he's going to go downstairs and this is going to be the subject of breakfast conversation. The two of us, in our underwear, in the same bedroom."

"And in the same bed," he said. "We could always crawl back under the covers and really mess with their heads," Jake offered. She sent him a withering look and he held up his hands in mock surrender. "Bad joke. Sorry."

With a low growl, Caley scrambled to her feet and tossed the comforter aside. "You haven't changed at all, Jake Burton. Everything is always a joke to you. You never take anything seriously."

Jake watched as she searched for her pants. "Don't get your panties in a twist. I'll explain the mistake. Although I'm not going to give them all the details."

"The state of my panties is none of your business. And I don't remember any of the details. Why? Because I was asleep."

Jake laughed. To think he'd dreaded seeing her again, knowing how uncomfortable it might be. But they'd slipped right back into their normal dynamic. Jake swung his legs over the side of the bed, fighting the urge to grab her arm and pull her back on top of him, to remind her of her reaction to his kiss.

There had always been a heat between them, an attraction that he'd been reluctant to act upon. She'd always been too young, too naive. And he'd known she was in love with him, so it could only end badly. He'd thought he'd done the honorable thing that night so long ago, the night she'd offered up her virginity for his taking.

His rejection obviously still stung. If not that, what else could she possibly be angry about? "If you're still angry about—"

Caley gasped, then threw a shoe at him. "I'm not angry about that. Just forget about that. I was young and stupid and I've slept with plenty of men since then and all of them much better lovers than you could have possibly been. Some women might find you attractive, but not me."

Her phone rang for a fourth time. Jake jumped off the bed and caught her arm, then pulled her against him. Without a second thought, he brought his mouth down on hers and kissed her, deeply and thoroughly. He felt her soften in his arms and when her knees buckled, Jake grabbed her waist to steady her.

When he finally drew back, her face was flushed and her eyes closed. He felt his own reaction in his boxers, the desire returning immediately. This was going to be one helluva week if this was how they were starting, he mused. There had always been a sexual curiosity between them. Maybe it was time to satisfy it.

"Are you going to answer that?" he asked.

"It can wait," Caley replied breathlessly.

"Yeah," he murmured, "that's what I thought." Nothing had changed. He wanted her just as much as he always had.

Caley opened her eyes and stared at him, a sigh slipping from her lips. "I-I'd better get dressed. Everyone is going to be expecting us at breakfast." She quickly grabbed her overnight bag and rushed to the adjoining bathroom, then slammed the door behind her.

Jake sat down on the bed and smiled. This was a start and maybe that was all he could hope for. He glanced around the room, grabbed his jeans from the bedpost and tugged them on. He found a clean T-shirt in his duffel and pulled it over his head. He'd find a way to continue what they'd begun later in the day.

When he got downstairs, the huge kitchen was filled with people. Caley's mother, Jean, was busy at the stove, preparing pancakes for her family. Her eldest, Evan, was just a year older than Jake, but already had a wife and three children. After Caley came Adam and Emma, followed by Teddy, who would graduate from high school in June. Evan was reading the sports section and discussing the Bulls game with Jake's younger brother Brett.

"Good morning, everyone," Jake said, taking the first empty spot at the huge table.

"Sausage or bacon, dear?" Jean called.

"Bacon," Jake said. A moment later, a plate was dropped in front of him. He reached out for the lazy Susan, which held utensils, napkins, butter and syrup.

The Lambert house was so much like his own that he felt at home at their table. He couldn't remember the number of meals that he'd eaten in their kitchen, usually with several of his siblings. Jean and Jake's mother, Fran, never bothered to sort out their respective children at mealtime. Whoever was sitting at the table at the beginning of a meal got fed, no matter which family they belonged to.

Jake had just dug into his pancakes when Teddy walked in the back door, covered in snow and carrying an armload of firewood. He sent Jake a knowing smile, then dropped the wood next to the door. "Morning, Jake. How'd you sleep?"

"Teddy, I want you to take some firewood over to Ellis and Fran's house," Jean said. "Load a bunch in the back of your truck. We have plenty. Jake can help you load it."

Teddy grinned. "Oh, I think he might be too tired to load firewood, Ma. So didja get much sleep last night, Jake?"

"I've been meaning to get a new mattress for that bed," Jean said. "It wasn't too lumpy, was it?"

"Not lumpy," Teddy said. "Maybe a little crowded."

Caley's mother scowled. "Teddy, what are you talking about?"

The entire group turned to hear Teddy's response. "Caley was sleeping with Jake."

Jean gasped. "Caley's home? When did she get in?"

"At about three in the morning."

They all turned again, this time to Caley, who stood in the doorway of the kitchen. She was dressed in a bulky wool sweater a shade of blue that complemented her eyes. Faded jeans hugged her long legs and slender hips.

"I thought I was crawling into bed with Emma," she explained. "It was a mistake. And nothing happened."

"Emma's staying at the inn," Jean said, bustling over to give her daughter a huge hug. She stepped back. "That's right, you don't know the big news, do you?"

"Jake told me," Caley replied. "Sam and Emma. Who would have thought?" She cleared her throat and looked at the curious gazes of her siblings. "Nothing happened. It was a mistake."

"Of course nothing happened," Jean said. "You two are like oil and water." She kissed Caley's cheek and smiled at Jake. "How could you possibly mistake Jake for Emma?"

"He had the covers over his head," Caley explained.

"Well, since I don't have to worry about you two getting cozy, maybe I should just have you bunk together for the rest of the week," Jean teased. "Oh, and Emma is going to ask you to be her maid of honor, darling. I hope you'll say yes. Bacon or sausage?"

"I'll just have the pancakes," Caley said, glancing across the table at Jake. "And you don't have to worry about me. I booked a room at the inn." She paused. "I'll be able to help Emma out. Since I'm her maid of honor. And Jake can have Emma's room all to himself."

Caley searched for a spot at the table and Adam moved his seat to make a space between himself and Jake. Caley reluctantly retrieved a chair and sat down. Her mother put a plate down in front of her and Jake picked up the pitcher of orange juice and poured her a glass. He held it out and she hesitantly took it and set it beside her plate.

They ate in silence, the both of them pretending to listen to the conversation around them. Jake's foot brushed against hers and she coughed on the orange juice she was drinking.

It was so nice to be able to touch her, Jake mused.

He felt her hand push his leg away and he reached beneath the table to grab it, weaving his fingers through hers. Her eyes grew wide as his thumb rested on her wrist, just over her pulse point.

"What's the schedule for today?" Caley asked, her voice cracking slightly.

"Emma's chosen a dress for you at the bridal shop in town and you need to go try it on this morning. The snow is getting deep. Adam will take you in his truck."

"I'll take Caley into town," Jake volunteered, giving her hand a squeeze. "I have some errands to run anyway."

"I can drive myself," Caley said, tugging her hand from his.

Jean smiled at Jake. "Thank you, dear. I knew I could count on you." She folded her hands in front of her, then looked back and forth between Jake and Caley. "It's so nice to see you two together again. How long has it been?"

"Eleven years," Caley said. She grabbed her plate and stood up. "I've got to make some calls. And I can drive myself to town. I have to check in at the inn before I go to the fitting." She sent Jake a cool look, then stalked out of the room.

Jake stood and carried his plate to the sink. "Not much has changed. Come on, Teddy, let's get that firewood loaded."

As they grabbed their jackets and walked out the back door, Teddy chuckled softly. "Oh, I think a lot has changed."

"And I'm not so sure you need help with the firewood," Jake replied.

"Sorry," Teddy murmured.

Jake used to be able to hide his feelings for Caley. But from the moment he woke that morning to find her wrapped around his body, Jake knew he wanted to explore those feelings. He and Caley weren't teenagers anymore, they were adults. And there were no rules keeping them apart. Now that there was time to test their attraction to each other, he planned to take full advantage of it.

2

THE GENTLE SNOWFALL increased in intensity throughout the early morning. Caley watched it from the window seat in her father's den. She'd been trying to work, making calls back and forth to the office and trying to send a report via a dial-up modem. She decided to wait until she had better Internet access at the inn and sent a text message to her assistant in the meantime.

Trying to concentrate on work had been impossible. Her mind kept returning to the bedroom upstairs and to the kiss that she and Jake had shared. A shiver skittered down her spine and she rubbed her arms to quell the goose bumps. It was usually so easy to focus on work and now just one silly kiss—two, really—had completely consumed her thoughts.

She closed her laptop and gathered up her things; she would check into the inn right after her fitting. But right now she had to concentrate on getting to her car, which was probably buried. She remembered Jake's offer of a ride, but thought it best not to tempt fate. It had been far too easy to kiss him. Given another chance, who knows what they might do?

Caley found a hodgepodge of winter outerwear in the hall closet and pulled on a jacket, boots, mittens and a cap. She tucked her phone into her pocket and trudged outside to shovel. She was glad for the distraction, for something productive to occupy her thoughts.

Other things had happened in that bed and she searched the haze of her memories for details. There had been a long, delicious dream in which Jake had finally succumbed to her charms. She'd spent most of her teenage years fantasizing about that moment when he'd pull her into his arms and kiss her, so it was no wonder that back in North Lake those thoughts had invaded her sleep again.

Yes, he'd kissed her. But the heavens hadn't opened and the angels hadn't sung. All right, a small chorus had made an appearance. After all, she'd have to be made of ice not to react.

As she started to shovel, she remembered the desire that had bubbled up inside of her the moment his lips touched hers. Caley had wanted him to continue, to make the kiss a beginning rather than an end. She'd longed for him to brush aside her clothes and kiss her naked skin, to pull her back to the bed and seduce her until she trembled at his touch.

She'd once fantasized that Jake was her Prince

Charming, pure and noble. Now, she saw him as a man with a killer smile and an incredible body and a way of looking at her that made her tingle all over.

She stepped back from her task and drew a deep breath, trying to calm her racing pulse. It probably wouldn't be difficult to let nature take its course. Jake had clearly seemed interested that morning— more than interested, if what was going on beneath his boxers was any indication. And it wasn't as though she'd be seducing a complete stranger. She'd been so curious for so long, now why not enjoy Jake while she could?

She'd left New York with her life in turmoil, searching for the key to her happiness. Sleeping with Jake might make her happy for the short term. Though she'd insulted his prowess in bed, Caley suspected that she'd thoroughly enjoy being seduced by him. He was different now. A shiver skittered down her spine. He was definitely a man—a very sexy, handsome, powerful man.

She sighed, her breath clouding in front of her face. Her rational mind told her she didn't need to add any more complications to her life. But sleeping with Jake might not be complicated so much as exciting and dangerous and wildly satisfying. Closing her eyes, she took another deep breath. Was it really Jake that she wanted or just someone—anyone—who made her feel better about her life?

Caley had nearly cleared one wheel of the car when Jake pulled up in an SUV. He beeped the horn at her, then rolled down the window and grinned. "Get in," he said. "I'll take you to town. You'll never get that car dug out by yourself."

Caley held her breath as she stared at him. He'd looked handsome that morning, dressed in only his boxers, his hair mussed by sleep and a scruffy day-old beard darkening his jaw. Now, he looked almost irresistible. Her gaze dropped to his mouth and she wondered when she'd kiss him next. Caley turned back to her shoveling, afraid that she hadn't the power to resist him. "I—I can drive myself."

"Come on, Caley. You're not going to get the car out in any kind of reasonable time."

She glanced over her shoulder, ready to concede defeat on both the car and her immunity to his charm. Jake jumped out of the SUV, grabbed the shovel, stuck it into a snowdrift and held out his hand. "Come on."

Caley stared down at his fingers, long and tapered. A memory drifted through her mind, hazy but real. He'd touched her that morning. It hadn't been part of her dream. His fingers had danced over her skin and his touch had made her body come alive.

Hesitantly, she placed her hand in his and he led her to his SUV. He opened the passenger-side door and helped her inside, then circled around to get in behind the wheel. In the end, she really didn't want to drive into town on her own, especially along curvy West Shore Road. All it would take was a skid into the ditch and she'd have to listen to Jake's repeated "I told you so."

"Buckle up," he said.

Caley turned to him. "I think we need to get one thing clear. I'm not in love with you anymore. Any crush I might have had as a teenager is long gone. So don't act like you have me wrapped around your little finger, because you don't."

Caley turned to stare out the window, embarrassed by her sudden outburst. She was usually so careful about her choice of words. What was it about Jake that made her act like a petulant teenager? Why did he always have to challenge her?

Jake threw the truck into gear and headed up the hill to the end of the driveway. The SUV easily handled the deep drifts and the slippery conditions. But she wasn't about to give Jake the satisfaction of being right.

"You were in love with me?" he asked. "When exactly was that?"

"Years ago," she murmured. "For about a week. It's all a very vague memory."

"So you aren't even slightly attracted to me now?" A grin quirked at the corners of his mouth.

"No," she lied.

He considered her answer for a long moment. "Too bad. Because I'm still kind of attracted to you. Yeah, I know. Surprising, right?"

"Still?" Caley asked, stunned by his admission.

"Yeah, still. Hey, I always thought you were hot."

Caley laughed out loud at the audacity of his comment. "Please," she said.

"No, I did. I do. Come on, Caley, look at yourself. A guy would have to be crazy to think otherwise. You're beautiful and sophisticated and smart."

She wasn't sure whether he was teasing her or telling the truth. But it did make her feel better. Caley smiled.

"All the guys were madly in love with you that summer before you left for college."

"Now you *are* lying. But go on."

"I told them you were taken."

She frowned at him. "But I wasn't. Why would you tell them that?"

"They were only looking for one thing and I just didn't want them putting the moves on you. I didn't think you were ready for that. And maybe I felt a little possessive."

"You were the reason I left for college a virgin."

"Believe me, I would have loved to help you out on that one, but I wasn't sure I'd be the right guy for the job." He paused. "I'd assume you solved that problem a while ago."

Caley giggled. "Are you asking if I'm a virgin? I'm twenty-eight years old."

"I was talking about finding the right guy. Teddy mentioned that you're living with some lawyer."

Caley opened her mouth, ready to tell him that Brian was probably moving his stuff out of their apartment as they spoke. But admitting that would leave her with no defense against seduction. "Yeah. We've been together for a couple years. What about you?"

Caley didn't want to hear the answer. She wanted to believe that the only woman on his mind was her. But that would be unrealistic. Jake was an attractive, successful man.

"No one special," he said. "I guess I was saving myself for you."

She bit her bottom lip, focusing on the road ahead. Why did he say things like that? Was he testing her? Jake had always enjoyed teasing her, but this was different. It was as if he was daring her to take his words seriously.

They drove for a long while in silence. She took out her cell phone and began to text another message to her assistant.

"Do you take that thing with you everywhere?"

"I need to be available. People are counting on me."

"The rats would continue to race even if you weren't running alongside them. Take a break. You're supposed to be on vacation."

"Partners don't ever really go on vacation," she said. Still, she tucked the phone back into her pocket, leaving the message unfinished.

A question nagged at Caley's brain, a question she never thought she'd have the nerve or the opportunity to ask. But it needed to be answered. "If you were so attracted to me, then why did you turn me down that night?"

He smiled, but kept his gaze fixed on the road ahead. "You'd just turned eighteen. I was almost twenty. I didn't think it was the right time. It was your first time and I figured that should be perfect. I wasn't sure I would be able to do that for you." He glanced over at her. "I did you a big favor, Caley. I didn't want you to regret your first experience."

Caley sat back in the seat and stared out the window. Though his words did a bit to soothe the memory of her humiliation, she had a hard time believing Jake was that noble. "I was devastated," she said.

He reached over and slipped his hand around her nape. Her pulse quickened and Caley felt a rush of desire as his fingers tangled in her hair. "I'm sorry," he replied, gently forcing her to look at him. "But, if it will make you feel better, I'd be glad to do the job now."

She saw the wry grin on his face and Caley couldn't help but laugh. "I'll let you know."

"Hey, I've been told I do an admirable job in the sack."

"That's because all the women you sleep with are too blinded by your pretty face. They'd say anything to keep you in their beds."

Jake pulled the truck over to the edge of the road and threw it out of gear. "My charm worked pretty well on you this morning."

"I was asleep."

"You said my name."

She shrugged, trying to maintain a cool facade. It wasn't working. Her hands were trembling and she felt a little light-headed. "Well, it won't work anymore. Go ahead. Kiss me. You'll see, I won't have any reaction." It was a feeble challenge and she knew he could see right through it. But she didn't care. She wanted to kiss him again and she couldn't wait any longer.

To her surprise, he accepted her challenge. Before she could even take a breath, he grabbed her face between his hands and kissed her. At first, the kiss was full of frustration. But then, he softened his touch and slipped his tongue between her lips.

Caley grabbed the front of his jacket and pulled him toward her, until he was sprawled across the console, his hands furrowed through her hair. They couldn't seem to get close enough, tearing at each other's clothes, searching for something more to touch. Though she knew she ought to put a stop to it, the taste of him, the feel of his body against hers was exhilarating, like some crazy carnival ride that frightened her and thrilled her all at once.

He slipped his hand under the waist of her pants and clutched her backside, pulling her hips against his. He was aroused and Caley enjoyed the fact that he couldn't resist her any more than she could resist him.

"What the hell are you doing to me?" he murmured, his breath warm against her ear. "You have a boyfriend. You're living with him."

"We broke up," she murmured, nuzzling her face into the curve of his neck.

Jake grabbed her shoulders and pushed her back, staring down into her eyes. "Don't play games with me, Caley."

"I'm not. I swear, we broke up. It's over."

Jake dragged his thumb over her bottom lip. "Can we just stop pretending then? I'm man enough to admit that I want you. And I think you want me, right?"

"Maybe," Caley murmured.

"Not maybe," he said, shaking his head.

"All right. I'll admit that there is an interesting attraction between us."

"So what are we going to do about it?"

Caley frowned. "I don't know. It could be complicated."

He drew back, then grinned. "When you figure out what you want, you let me know," he said.

Caley gasped softly. Was that it? Wasn't he supposed to pull her into his arms and kiss away all her doubts? Or seduce her without any regard to her reservations? He wasn't supposed to drop the ball back in her court!

"I will," Caley said softly.

Jake straightened, sliding back behind the wheel. "We should probably get going."

When they reached the small bridal shop in the village, Jake parked, then hopped out and circled around the front to open her door. The Burton boys had always had impeccable manners.

"Watch out," he said, as he grabbed her waist. "It's slippery beneath this snow." His hands lingered on her hips as his gaze fell to her mouth.

They stood there for a long moment, frozen in place, their breath clouding between them. Then Caley pushed up on her toes and touched her lips to his. "I'm not playing games with you," she whispered. "I just felt like kissing you again."

"I know how that feels," he replied. His arms slipped around her waist and he pulled her body against his. Jake brought his hands up to her face and gently cupped her cheeks as he returned the kiss. But the sound of laughter brought an end to their momentary pleasure. Caley turned to watch two teenage girls in the midst of a snowball fight.

"It's no one," he whispered, his breath warm against her ear.

"If we do this, we can't let anyone know," she said.

"I never kiss and tell," he said.

"I'm serious. It has to stay just between us. And it has to be just sex. Nothing more."

"Friends with benefits?" he asked.

She nodded. "I'll be right back," she said, glancing over at the bridal shop.

"I'll come in and wait," he said.

"Is that wise?" she asked.

"I'm not going to seduce you in a public place," he said. "And I don't think Miss Belle is going to go running to our parents to tell on us."

He followed her to the door, then pulled it open for her, placing his hand on the small of her back as she stepped inside. It was a simple gesture, but Caley realized that Jake was taking any opportunity offered to touch her.

The owner of the shop, Miss Belle, greeted them both, then drew Caley along to the fitting rooms in the back. She stopped and turned to Jake, motioning to him. "Are you coming, too?"

"Oh, no," Caley said. "He's not my—well, he's just a— I don't think he'd be interested."

"I'll come," Jake said, sending Caley a playful grin. "I'm very interested."

Caley took the dress into the fitting room and slipped out of her clothes. Though the dress didn't look like much on the hanger, when she put it on it was another story. The silky fabric clung to every curve of her body; the modest neckline plunged to a deep V in the back; the long sleeves fitted to her arms. She slipped out of her bra and then turned to examine the rear view. Emma had gotten the sizing perfect and had chosen a dress that would look stunning for an evening wedding.

Caley pulled open the fitting room door and stepped out. Jake had been sitting on a bench and the moment he saw her, he quickly stood, a tiny gasp slipping from his lips.

"Wow," he murmured. "That's some dress."

Caley smoothed her hands over her hips as she turned. "It is nice, isn't it?"

"Are you wearing underwear?"

She gave him a stern look. "It's too clingy."

"So, you're not going to wear underwear. Where the hell am I supposed to put my hands when we dance?" he asked. "This is going to be a problem."

"Are we going to dance?"

"You're the maid of honor and I'm the best man. I think it's a rule than we take at least one turn around the floor."

Miss Belle hurried up and studied Caley critically. "We'll bring the sleeves up a bit. I'd assume you plan to go…without?" She pointed to Caley's chest.

"Do I have a choice?" Caley asked.

"Well, we have the stick-ons."

"Can we see some of those?" Jake asked, a worried expression on his face.

Caley shook her head. "This will be fine."

Miss Belle held out a shoebox. "Try the shoes so I can check the hem."

Caley grabbed a shoe from the box and tried to put it on, but couldn't keep her balance in the long dress. Jake slipped his hands around her waist and steadied her as she put on the dyed-to-match pumps.

"Perfect," the shopkeeper said. "I'll be right back." Miss Belle hurried off to answer the phone, leaving Jake and Caley alone at the rear of the shop.

"Perfect," Jake repeated.

"Stop saying things like that to me," she murmured. "Sometimes I feel like you're playing with me."

He shook his head. "It's how we are, Caley. It's how we've always been."

She turned and walked back to the fitting room, and Jake followed close on her heels. When she stepped inside, Caley tried to close the door behind her, but Jake slipped inside, then leaned back against the door.

"In all the time that I've known you, have I ever lied to you?" Jake asked.

Caley stared at her fingernails. Until that night of her eighteenth birthday, Jake had been the one person she knew she could count on for unadulterated honesty. "I don't think so."

"Who told you to take the toilet paper out of your bra the night of the Fourth of July dance at the park? Who told you you looked like a giraffe when you started wearing those platform shoes? Who told you not to go out with Jeff Winslow because all he wanted to do was feel you up?"

"You did," Caley said. "But I went out with Jeff Winslow anyway. Of course, he did try to feel me up."

"See?"

"Just because you never lie to me doesn't mean that you don't have the capacity to hurt me."

He took a step toward her, then reached out and touched her cheek. "Does that hurt?"

Caley drew a shaky breath. It felt so good to have him touch her, his fingertips leaving a warm imprint on her skin. She shook her head. This time she wouldn't make it so easy for him. This time she'd resist him.

Jake took another step closer and kissed her softly on the forehead. "How about that? Tell me it feels good."

She swallowed hard, then sighed deeply as he kissed her temple. Did she have the strength? And was it wise to try and resist? It really didn't seem worth the effort. "Yes," she said. "It feels good."

He hooked his finger beneath her chin and tipped her gaze up to meet his. And then he kissed her, his tongue teasing at her lips before gently invading her mouth. But it wasn't like the kiss in the truck. This kiss was slow and sensuous, meant to melt all her resolve. Caley wrapped her arms around his neck and surrendered, enjoying the rush of heat that coursed through her body.

His hands slid down her waist to her hips, then circled to smooth over her back, left bare by the cut of the dress. Caley's mind whirled as she tried to remember every detail of the kiss, forcing herself not to slip into some hazy state of desire. But in the end, it was impossible to maintain her composure. Jake seemed determined to prove that he was quite possibly the best kisser in the entire world.

When his hand moved to her breast, she moaned softly. He grazed his thumb across her nipple, bringing it to a hard peak, sending a wild wave of pleasure coursing through her. When he finally drew back, Caley was dizzy with excitement. Her breath was coming in quick gasps and her pulse was pounding in her head.

"If that ever stops feeling good, you just let me know and I'll stop," Jake whispered. He kissed the tip of her nose, then walked out of the fitting room, closing the door behind him.

Caley stumbled back until she leaned against the mirrored wall for support. Her trembling fingers touched her lips and she felt a smile growing there.

After all these years, it was hard to believe that all her fantasies about Jake might just come true.

There was something powerful pulsing between them and it didn't look like either one of them had the capacity—or the will—to stop it. And that made it all the more exciting—and dangerous.

"THE BURTBERT SNOW BOWL begins in fifteen minutes!" Brett·called.

Jake and Sam looked over their shoulders at their brother and gave him a wave. "We'll be ready," Jake shouted.

They sat on the stairs that, in the summer, led down to the dock and the beach they shared with the Lamberts. The lake was frozen over and covered with snow, but Teddy Lambert had cleared an area big enough for skating or a pick-up hockey game.

Jake stretched his legs out in front of him and watched the last of the snowflakes drift lazily through the air. The storm was over and everything was covered with a sparkly powder. "So you're getting married."

Sam smiled as he traced a pattern in the snow with a stick. "That's what I hear."

"I gotta tell you, Sam, I was surprised when I heard you were engaged to Emma. But then when I heard you were getting married so quickly, I was kinda shocked. A month and a half is a pretty short engagement, don't you think?"

"Maybe."

"How much time have you two really spent together?"

Sam shrugged. "Three summers, here at the lake house. And then I visited her in Boston over Thanksgiving and we got together during Christmas break in Chicago and we just decided we didn't want to be apart anymore."

"Why not live together then?" Jake asked. "Give yourself some more time."

"Because Emma wants to get married," Sam said.

"What do you want?"

"Why so many questions?" Sam asked, a hint of irritation creeping into his voice.

"That's my job as your best man. To be sure you're making the best choices."

"I want what Emma wants. I want to make her happy," Sam said.

Jake hadn't been thrilled when he heard about his little brother's plans to get married, but he chalked that up to surprise. But now that he had a chance to spend some time with Sam and talk to him, Jake realized that twenty-one was far too young to take such a giant step.

He'd spent the last ten years working his way through a variety of females, trying to figure out what made them tick, enjoying the full spectrum of pleasures in their beds. But it was only in the past year that he'd really come to understand what he needed in a relationship and the kind of woman he wanted to spend his life with. Sam hadn't even started on that journey and already he was tying himself down. How could anyone know they were in love at that age? Neither Sam nor Emma had experienced anything of the world yet.

"You're not even finished with college," Jake murmured.

"Emma graduates in the spring and she's just got a few independent study courses, so she'll be spending more time in Chicago. I'll finish at Northwestern at Christmas next year and then I'm thinking about law school. If we get married, we can start planning our lives together—and she can support me while I'm getting my law degree."

"You can do all that without getting married," Jake said.

Sam groaned, then leaned back on his elbows, staring out at the wide landscape of the lake. "Maybe I should have asked Brett to be my best man. Or Emma's brother Teddy."

"Marriage is a big step, Sam. You have to get married for the right reasons."

"What reasons would those be?"

"Because you can't imagine living without her. Because every time you look at her, you have to touch her, just to make sure she's real and she's yours. Because she's the first thing you think about in the morning when you get up and the last thing you think about before you go to sleep."

Jake drew a deep breath. This was the sum total of his knowledge about living happily ever after. It was what he'd decided it would take to tempt him into settling down for the rest of his life. And oddly enough, Caley seemed to meet all those requirements.

A shiver skittered down his spine. Women were supposed to confuse lust and love, not men. Still, Jake couldn't ignore his feelings. Things weren't the same as when they were kids. There was something deeper…something stronger drawing them together now.

He glanced over at Sam. "I'd hate to think you're doing this to please Mrs. Lambert and our mother. All that Burtbert shit is really silly. We can still be one big family, even if we aren't technically related."

"It's not about that," Sam said.

"What is it, then?"

"We just want to start our lives together."

"I know it seems like you'll never get enough of her, but that kind of desire doesn't last. It's not all about sex," Jake said. "There has to be something more."

"Oh, we haven't had sex," Sam said. "Emma wanted to wait until we got married."

Jake gasped. "You haven't— I mean, not even a little?"

"Well, a little. But not the whole way."

Jake groaned and buried his face in his hands. "How can you possibly make a decision about the rest of your life when you don't even know if you're compatible in the bedroom?"

"Lots of people wait," he said. "And it's not like I haven't done it. And Emma has, too. We just haven't done it together."

"Well, maybe you should," Jake said. "Just to make sure." Hell, he'd never even tried to regulate his own desires for women—and since Caley had arrived back in town, Jake didn't even feel in control of his libido. How did a guy just put those feelings on the back burner? Wasn't it scientifically proven that abstaining wasn't good for the male body?

He took a deep breath. "Why not just wait a little longer? It couldn't hurt."

"I love her," Sam said. "And she loves me."

"I love Emma, too," Jake said. "And Caley and Teddy and Adam and Evan. The Lamberts are like our family." Jake sighed softly, searching for another argument that made sense. Who was he to try to explain what went on between a man and a woman? Hell, he couldn't begin to fathom his obsessive attraction to Caley. All he knew was that it felt good when he was with her, so good that he never wanted to let her go.

He pushed to his feet and offered his little brother

a hand. "Come on. If I know Brett, he's going to want to strategize before we get the game going. The last time we played football with the Lamberts, they beat us bad. They've got Evan's wife now and she's gone through natural childbirth three times. She's no wuss."

"And Caley plays like a guy," Sam said.

"Don't worry about Caley, I can handle her. You just take care of Emma."

Sam grinned. "Until we're married, she's still a Lambert. And the enemy."

They walked up to the lawn, now covered in a foot of powdery snow. After a few minutes, all the players were congregated at the center of the field. When Jake saw Caley, he gave her a wave and she returned his greeting with a hesitant smile. She looked so cute bundled up against the cold that it didn't take more than a moment for his mind to begin a fantasy of slowly peeling off all those layers of clothes. Jake drew a sharp breath and closed his eyes. Now was not the time to think about getting naked with Caley!

Once everyone was gathered, Brett raised his hand. "Welcome to the first, and possibly only, Burtbert Snow Bowl. In the tradition of our annual summer Toilet Bowl football game, we have decided to bring back the time-honored trophy." He pulled a toilet plunger from behind his back and everyone laughed and clapped, surprised to see the trophy after so long.

"The last time this was awarded was eleven years

ago last summer and, according to the inscription, it was won by the Lamberts."

"On a touchdown run by Caley," Jake said. He looked at her. "Remember? Adam threw you the ball and you just took off down the field. No one could catch you."

She gave him an odd look. "I don't remember that."

Jake shrugged. "I do. It was a great play."

He slowly walked around the perimeter of the crowd as Brett went over the rules, stopping when he stood behind Caley. His gaze fixed on Sam and Emma. "They look happy," he murmured. "What do you think?"

Caley glanced over her shoulder at him. "Yes," she replied.

Brett pointed to the list of winners, written on the wooden handle with a marker. "Our captains today will be Sam and Emma. By my count, we've got even teams with Evan's wife, Marianne, and Ann's husband, John, so no one has to sit out."

Teddy disagreed. "We have three guys and three girls and you've got four guys and two girls. You call that even?"

"John just had knee surgery last year," Brett said. "And Marianne played college soccer. I'd say it's even."

The coin was flipped and the game began. Brett played quarterback for the Burton team and when he went out for a long pass to Ann, Caley stepped out in front of her and snagged an interception.

She started off down the sideline and Jake took off after her, making up the distance between them in a few seconds. He grabbed Caley around the waist and picked her up off her feet, then fell into the snow near the goal line, taking the impact with his body.

They'd played in this rough-and-tumble fashion when they were kids and back then it had been fun. But now, lying beneath Caley, her body stretched out on top of his, the game had taken on a sexual element.

"This is supposed to be touch football!" she cried.

"And I'm touching you," Jake murmured. "Although not the way I'd like to touch you." He rolled Caley beneath him, pinning her body to the ground with his. "We have to talk," he said softly.

She wriggled beneath him, trying to escape. "If you think you can convince me to throw this game," she whispered, "just because you kissed me then—"

"Later," he replied as he saw Brett approach. Jake rolled off her and helped her up and then brushed the snow off her backside, before sending her across the scrimmage line to her team. "Good catch," he shouted.

A change of possession put Jake on offense and he took a handoff from Brett and headed down the field. He saw Caley coming toward him and he knew she was prepared to hit him hard. That's what he liked about Caley. She never backed off from a challenge. But instead of running away, he waited, slowing his run until she caught up.

Jake feinted to the left, then the right, but Caley surprised him by countering his moves. When Jake realized he wasn't going to shake her, he bent over, grabbed her around the waist and carried her toward the end zone with him. But Caley knocked the ball out of his hand as he ran.

"Fumble!" she shouted.

Teddy was right behind them and he picked up the ball and started toward the other end zone. Jake turned and dropped Caley into the snow, then ran after Teddy, but Caley grabbed his leg and pulled him down. When he was lying on his stomach in the snow, she crawled on top of him, straddling his hips, and watched as Teddy scored.

She bounced up and down as she cheered for her brother, the movement causing a definite reaction on his part. Cursing softly, Jake rolled over and dumped her into the snow, picking up a handful and rubbing it in her face.

"You are such a bad sport," Caley cried, grabbing a fistful of snow and throwing it at him. She wrestled him to his back, pinning his arms on either side of his head.

"Kiss me," he murmured.

Caley frowned. "Not here. Everyone will see."

Jake brushed the snow out of her hair. "Where? When?"

"Later," Caley said. "After dinner."

"Meet me at the boathouse," he said.

Caley shook her head, then got to her feet, running back to her team. She turned around and looked back at him once, smiling, teasingly taunting him. "You're gonna lo-ose," she sang. "You're gonna lo-ose."

She did a little dance, wiggling her backside, and Jake chuckled. God, she was sexy. As he watched her walk away, he thought about what it would be like to have an entire night alone with her. To have all the time in the world to seduce her. To slowly undress her and touch her body and make her moan with pleasure. She'd been the stuff of his adolescent fantasies. But now, the things he dreamed about doing with her—to her—weren't things he could have even imagined back then.

"Jake!"

He glanced up to see Brett staring at him. "Look alive," his brother shouted. "Keep your head in the game."

They played for exactly an hour and, in the end, the trophy went to the Lambert family on a last-minute touchdown pass from Evan to his wife, Marianne.

As they walked back up to the house, Jake lagged behind, his gaze fixed on Caley. He wondered how things might have been between them if he had accepted her offer that night eleven years ago. Would they be here, in the same place, still lusting after each other? Or might they look at each other with embarrassment or regret rather than anticipation and excitement?

Maybe things had worked out exactly as they were supposed to that summer. But what happened between them this week was still in the hands of fate. And it would either begin or end in the boat-house tonight.

DINNER WAS A BOISTEROUS EVENT with both families sharing chili and corn bread in the Burtons' huge family room. After dinner, Jake and Caley joined Sam and Emma in a game of Monopoly, but Caley could barely concentrate. Jake had taken to playing a game of footsie beneath the table, running his stocking foot over hers in a very seductive manner.

Caley kept her gaze focused on the board, trying to control her wildly beating heart. There had been men in her life who had touched her in the most intimate of ways and she'd barely reacted. All Jake had to do was rub her foot and she felt like tearing his clothes off and jumping his bones.

"Park Place," Sam said as Emma landed on his property. "Let's see. That will be twelve hundred dollars, please."

Jake chuckled as he scrutinized Sam's stash of cash. "Looks like you almost have enough for that motorcycle you want to buy."

Sam shot his brother a cold look and Emma immediately frowned. "What motorcycle?"

"Sam's going to buy a motorcycle after you get married," Jake said as he straightened his property cards. "Our mother wouldn't let him, but once he's married, she can't say anything since you'd be in charge." He fixed Emma with an inquisitive gaze, waiting for her response.

Caley thought it was an odd turn in the conversation. She sent him a frown and he just smiled and began to count his money.

"You can't get a motorcycle," Emma said. "They're dangerous. I won't let you."

"But, Em, it would be practical. We can't afford two cars. And the gas would be cheap."

"No," Emma said stubbornly. "I won't allow it."

Sam straightened, his expression growing petulant. "What is that supposed to mean, you won't allow it? You're not my mother."

"Sam should be able to make his own decisions," Jake murmured.

Caley gave him a swift kick beneath the table and he winced.

"Ow!" he cried. Sam and Emma looked at him and he forced a smile. "Cramp. To much football in the snow." He snatched up his money and handed it to Caley. "I'm going to cash out now."

Caley looked back and forth between the glowering expressions on Sam's and Emma's faces to the smug smile on Jake's. He'd started this argument on purpose. "So am I," Caley said.

"Jake is right," Sam countered. "I'm an adult. I should be able to do what I want."

"Who's going to pay for this motorcycle?" Emma said. "Not me. And if you think you're going to use any of our wedding money, you'd better think again."

Caley quickly stood and followed Jake to the kitchen. He set his glass in the sink, then called out to his parents, who were playing cards with Caley's mother and father. "I'm going to go down to the boathouse and see if I can get the heat going. We're going to need the extra room."

"And I'm going to head back to the inn," Caley said. "I have to make some calls. I'll see you all tomorrow." Their mutual exit caused no undue interest. Jake helped her on with her jacket and they walked out the front door together.

When they got outside, he grabbed her hand and drew her along with him, toward the path down to the lake. "Jake, maybe we should— Where are we going?"

"The boathouse. I could use some help getting the heat going. You can hold my tools."

Caley laughed, then fell into step beside him. The crisp night air heightened her senses and she felt her heart skip, knowing what would happen once they were alone. Caley had never considered herself a very passionate woman. She'd always been able to control her desire. But with Jake, she seemed to be constantly fixated on sex.

Though she had good intentions of playing it cool, everything fell apart the moment he touched her. Her rational side could come up with an entire list of reasons why she shouldn't sleep with Jake. But then her pulse began pounding and she felt a tiny bit light-headed and her brain stopped working entirely. It felt good to just let go, to feel something so strongly that it completely consumed her. She hadn't felt like this since that night with Jake on the beach eleven years ago.

But was she really ready to do this? For the past few months, she'd felt an emptiness inside her, as if her life had ceased to make her happy. It would be easy to fill that emptiness with Jake. And maybe she would feel better for a while. Still, Caley didn't want to believe that she needed a man to be happy. She probably just needed really good sex.

At least she was now old enough to know the difference between desire and love. If she did surrender to physical attraction, Caley would be able to control her emotions. Jake was the last person she would allow herself to love. In truth, he was the only man she'd known who had the capacity to break her heart. And that made him dangerous.

And yet, she wasn't afraid. Instead, she felt liberated. She could finally act on her desire for Jake and explore just how deep it ran. She didn't have to pretend anymore. He wanted her and she wanted him, and neither one of them had to deny it.

The shadow of the Burtons' boathouse, built into the slope of the shoreline, loomed at the edge of the lake. The lower level held the Burtons' small sailboat and their vintage motorboat, but the upper level was a small apartment that they often used for guests. It was fully furnished with a bed and a sofa and a small kitchen and bath. The windows had been shuttered for the winter, giving the place a cold and uninviting look.

Jake held her hand as she carefully climbed the snow-covered stairs. Caley glanced back over her shoulder to see the trail of their footprints in the moonlight. "They're going to know we were out here together," she said.

"I just asked you to give me a hand," Jake said. "It was a perfectly innocent request."

Caley took a ragged breath and clenched her fingers inside her jacket pocket. Just the thought of running her hands over his body, of having the freedom to touch him, to undress him, made her mind spin. She knew what would happen when they were alone and she wasn't afraid. All she could feel was an overwhelming anticipation.

When they reached the landing, Jake pushed the door open and then walked inside. She followed and heard the door shut behind her. The moment it did, Caley felt his hands on her face. His lips met hers and a heartbeat later they were lost in a deep and stirring kiss.

"I've been thinking about you all day," he murmured against her mouth.

"What were you thinking?" she asked, her breath coming in quick gasps.

"About what would happen once we were alone again."

"Tell me," she said. "What did you imagine?"

It was so dark inside the boathouse that they couldn't see anything, but she could feel his heat against her body, his warm breath against her cheek. The lack of sight seemed to heighten all her other senses and she shivered as she felt his lips brush across her cold cheek.

"I imagined that you'd stand in front of me and slowly take all your clothes off. And then, I'd finally be able to touch you. And I'd be able to see if it felt as good as I dreamed it would."

Caley unzipped her jacket and let it fall to the floor behind her. Then, she pulled her sweater over her head and tossed it aside. She wore a thin T-shirt beneath, barely enough to protect her from the cold. But strangely, she didn't notice the temperature. Her heart was beating so fast that her skin didn't even prickle into goose bumps.

Jake reached out and ran his hand down her bare arm, then grabbed her hand and kissed the center of her palm. "Wait here," he murmured. "The circuit box is in the closet."

He disappeared into the darkness and Caley leaned back against the door, her heart pounding. She heard him fumbling around on the far side of the room and a moment later, a match flared. The flame illuminated the interior of the boathouse, casting wavering shadows on the walls. Jake lit a lantern and set it down on the bedside table. Then he turned to her, motioning her closer.

Caley rubbed her arms, suddenly feeling the cold along with a rush of nerves. It was easier in the dark, like a dream, two bodies connected only by touch. But now that she could see the bed, could look into Jake's eyes, it had all become very real.

"Let me see if I can get the heat going," he said. He walked past her to the opposite wall and leaned inside the closet. A switch clicked. A moment later, he bent over the radiator and nodded. "It's working."

Jake moved back toward her, taking off his jacket along the way. He was the boy she'd always known, every feature still there—the dark lashes and brows, the penetrating pale blue eyes, the straight nose and sensuous mouth. But with age, his features had become even more captivating, more compelling. She couldn't take her eyes off of him.

When he stood in front of her, Caley reached up and unbuttoned his shirt, exposing his skin to her touch. "What are we doing here?" she murmured, pressing her lips to his chest.

"I have no idea," Jake replied, "but I don't want to stop."

He smoothed his hands up her back and Caley shivered at the sensation of his touch. "This is going to be impossible," she murmured, nuzzling her face into his neck.

"We're in the same state, living minutes apart. How is that impossible?" He pulled her along to the bed. "We have heat and light and a comfortable bed. What happens here is just us, no one else. I promise."

"This could change everything," Caley said as he kissed her neck.

Jake grabbed her waist and they tumbled onto the bed, the covers cold on her bare skin. "I'm counting on that," he said.

Caley reached up to run her fingers through his dark hair and smiled. "You know, I really don't think we should do this. You're not ready and it wouldn't be right and I just don't think of you in that way."

He frowned, pushing back. "You don't?"

"I just don't have *those* kinds of feelings for you, Jake," she murmured, deepening her voice to make the imitation more obvious.

She watched as a slow smile broke across his face. He'd said those same words to her that night on the beach. "I lied," Jake said. "Believe me, I did have those feelings."

His admission stunned her. "Really?"

"For a long time."

"How long?"

"Remember that red striped bikini you had? You were fourteen that summer."

Caley nodded.

"Since then. I remember I saw you in that bikini and later that night I was thinking about you and your body and how smooth your skin was and how perfect your breasts were and then I—well, you know."

"I do?"

"What? You want me to say it? I pleasured myself as teenage boys do on occasion. Hey, grown men do it, too." He chuckled softly. "All I remember is, from that summer on, being around you was pure torture."

Caley smiled, satisfied with the admission. So the infatuation hadn't been unreciprocated. Oddly enough, that did make a difference. Why not make both of their fantasies come true? "So what else were you thinking about?" she asked as she dropped a line of kisses across his chest.

He pressed his mouth to her shoulder, gently biting as he kissed her. "I wasn't very experienced back then. I was still technically a virgin. But I thought about what you'd look like naked." Jake pulled up her T-shirt and trailed a line of kisses from her belly to a spot beneath her breasts.

Caley sat up and straddled his hips, then slowly pulled her T-shirt over her head. She remembered doing the same thing eleven years ago. But then, she'd been so nervous her heart nearly jumped out of her chest. Now, it seemed like the most natural thing in the world, to crave his touch, to offer him more.

Jake smiled as he reached out and cupped her breast in his hand, teasing at her nipple with his thumb. And then, in one easy motion, he sat up, wrapping his arms around her waist and pressing his mouth against her neck. He trailed kisses from her collarbone to her breasts as he unhooked her bra. Finally, he drew the hard nub of her nipple into his mouth.

She arched back, holding her breath as he pulled her back down with him. Caley remembered how fascinated she'd been with his body, watching it change from summer to summer as he slowly became a man. She was as desperate to touch it now as she had been then. Grabbing the front of his shirt, she worked at the remaining buttons, then brushed it off his shoulders until his chest was completely bare.

She drew back, staring at him as she tossed aside her bra. Her fingers lazily following the line of hair that ran from his collarbone to his belly. Now he was fully formed, his shoulders broad, his body lean and hard, a body only a woman could appreciate.

Caley bent forward and pressed a kiss to his chest, then gently sucked on his nipple. What began as curiosity had now taken on a very intimate feeling. He groaned softly, then murmured her name. A shiver skittered over her exposed skin. Her breath caught in her throat.

"Are you cold?" he asked.

"No," she lied.

He chuckled softly, grabbing her by the waist and pulling their bodies together in a warm embrace. They kissed for a long time, hands touching, mouths tasting. It was everything she'd always thought it would be, yet more. It wasn't just about sex, it was about…trust.

He ran his hands through her hair, then pressed his forehead against hers. "Spend the night with me."

"Not here."

"Where then?"

"At the inn. We'll have more privacy there."

"What about Emma?"

"Her room is on the second floor and mine's on

the third. There's a back stairway. I'll let you in and no one will know you're there."

Jake kissed her forehead, his lips warm and damp. "Have you talked to Emma yet? I mean, about the wedding."

Caley shook her head. "No. I told her I'd meet her for lunch tomorrow and I thought we'd have some time then."

"What do you think about this marriage? Do you think they're ready?"

"No!" Caley frowned, pushing up on her elbow. "Not at all. They're so young. I thought I was the only one who had concerns. Everyone is just so thrilled that our families will finally be related. But no one is even thinking about what will happen if the marriage doesn't work."

"I agree," Jake said. "I don't think they're ready."

Caley crossed her arms over his chest and stared into his eyes. "You started that fight between them on purpose, didn't you?"

"Someone has to shake some sense into them." He paused. "We need a plan. A coordinated effort between the two of us. If we go at it from both sides, maybe we'll be able to convince them to wait."

"I don't think they'll consider waiting. Everything is moving so fast and I'm sure they feel they'd be disappointing the families."

Jake reached out and brushed her hair away from

her temple, his gaze skimming over her face. "I talked to Sam this afternoon and he's just going along with what Emma wants."

Caley gasped. "You think she talked him into this?"

"Maybe. I can't imagine he really wants to get married. What guy in his right mind would want a wife at twenty-one?"

"Well, he's the one who asked her," Caley said. "If he didn't want to get married, why did he ask?"

"She probably pressured him," Jake said.

Caley pulled out of his embrace and sat up, stunned by his comment and eager to defend her sister. "Emma wouldn't do that."

"I'm just saying that usually women are the ones who press for the wedding," Jake said.

"And you come by this knowledge how?" Caley asked. "Have you been manipulated into an engagement recently?"

"No, just the opposite. Every woman I've ever met has had marriage in the back of her mind. Come on, even you've thought about it. Wondered what it would be like if you and I…you know."

Caley scrambled off the bed. Marrying Jake was the last thing on her mind! And if he thought she had any designs on his future, he was sadly mistaken. "I think this was a mistake," she murmured, crawling off the bed. She searched the floor for her bra and T-shirt.

"Come on, Caley, don't be mad. I didn't mean to imply that——"

"No, I understand," she said as she pulled the shirt over her head. "You just assumed I wanted more than just…sex." She drew a ragged breath, shoving her bra in her back pocket. "See, that's why we shouldn't do this. Unless we're agreed on the reasons, it's bound to get very messy."

"Is it?" he asked.

She snatched up her sweater from the floor and tugged it back over her head. "I have to go."

Jake sat up and reached for her, but she avoided his grasp. "Caley, come on. I was just teasing. I didn't mean anything by it."

She shook her head. "I do agree about Emma and Sam. They're too young. You and I don't even know what we want. How would they?"

Jake grabbed her hand. "I know what I want," he said.

She stared down at their fingers, intertwined so tightly that she couldn't tell his from hers. Caley fought the temptation to strip off her clothes again and just forget her fears. But if she jumped into bed with Jake tonight, there would be no going back. "I'll talk to Emma."

"When will I see you again?" Jake asked.

"You're going to see me all week."

"You know what I mean."

Caley bit her lower lip. "I don't know. Maybe we ought to forget this. It just makes things too complicated."

"I'm not sure I can," he replied.

"Try, Jake," she murmured. Caley walked to the door, then turned back to look at him. "Try really hard."

3

JAKE STEERED HIS SUV around a sharp curve on West Shore Road, his mother's grocery list clutched in his hand. He had an appointment for his tux fitting and then his mother wanted him to buy three "nice" chickens. He wasn't sure what qualified a chicken as nice, but he'd figure it out when he got to the grocery store.

The truck skidded and he took his foot off the accelerator, startled out of his thoughts. He'd gotten about two or three hours of sleep last night. The rest of his time in bed was spent trying to figure out just how he'd managed to screw things up with Caley.

Maybe the forces of the universe were sending him a message—don't mess with Caley Lambert. But though he'd considered heeding the message, his body didn't want to listen. Every time he came within ten feet of her, he found himself lost in another sexual fantasy.

This was his penance for keeping all his desire bottled up so long ago. It had increased over the years, like pressure in a simmering pot, until he was left with a need for Caley that threatened to boil over. He wanted to kiss her and touch her, to strip off her clothes and enjoy the pleasures of her body. He'd waited years and now that she was with him again, he wanted to make it happen.

But could it just be casual sex? Would he be able to enjoy the act and then walk away, no strings attached? From the moment he found her lying next to him in bed, he'd felt it. A deep-rooted connection, not diminished by time, but strengthened. She could never be just a physical release for him. Sex with Caley would have to mean something. But what?

Jake groaned, tightening his grip on the steering wheel. "It's just too complicated," he muttered, repeating her words. But it didn't seem at all complicated in his mind. In truth, seducing Caley felt like the most natural thing he'd ever done.

How long had he been searching for a woman just like her, a woman he could feel entirely comfortable with, a woman who didn't try to make herself into something she thought he wanted.

Jake had seen it all—the sexpot, the girl-next-door, the doting wife, the perfect mother of his children. They'd all tried to be something they weren't. He'd known Caley so long that she couldn't hide behind a facade. And if she tried, he would see right through it.

"Just take it slow," he told himself. He'd been able to resist her when he was younger and far less experienced with the opposite sex. It shouldn't be that difficult to bide his time.

His mind flashed back to an image of Caley, straddling his waist, tugging her T-shirt over her head. Jake's fingers twitched as he recalled the feel of her flesh beneath his hands, the taste of her skin, the scent of her hair. He drew a ragged breath and tried to banish the image from his mind and focus on something else.

He noticed a car ahead of him on the road and slowed, but the sedan wasn't moving. Instead, it was tilted at an odd angle. As he approached, Jake realized the car looked familiar—as did the figure standing at the front bumper. He carefully pulled over, then hopped out of the truck.

The moment Caley saw him, she turned away and shook her head. "Don't even say it," she muttered.

"Who taught you to drive?" he teased.

A reluctant smile broke across her face. "You did. Remember? You took me out in that old Cutlass you bought, then proceeded to yell at me for the entire lesson."

"You've forgotten everything I taught you, grasshopper," he teased, running his finger along her cheek. This time Jake fought the urge to kiss her and instead moved to the front of the car to examine the situation.

"We didn't cover ice and snow, if you recall."

"And how are you planning to get your car back on the road? By sheer force of will?"

"Maybe you could give me a push?"

"Not gonna work." Jake shoved his hands in his pockets. It took every ounce of his willpower just to keep from touching her. He never remembered her hold over him being this strong, but it must have been. How had he managed to say no the night of her eighteenth birthday? He shook his head. "It's going to take an hour of shoveling and two or three guys to get you out of this snowbank. I can go back home and get a chain and see if I can pull you out. Or I'll get Teddy and my brothers and we can shovel and push."

"My hero," Caley said with a mocking smile.

Jake's smile faded. He was short on sleep and tired of this game they played. Why did everything always have to be a challenge? "Am I? After last night, I thought you might not like me anymore."

Caley shrugged. "I like you. That's not going to change."

"I shouldn't have said those things about your sister."

She drew a deep breath and sighed, then reached out and touched his arm, as if to reassure herself that they were all right. "I'm as worried as you are. I'm having lunch with her later. I was hoping I'd get a better sense of what she's thinking."

"You know, they haven't had sex yet," Jake said.

Caley blinked, stunned by the revelation. "Really? They're both virgins?"

"No. They've both had sex, just not with each other. They're saving it for marriage."

"That changes everything," Caley said, her eyes wide. "I mean, I think it's an admirable concept, but it still worries me. Sex is an important part of a relationship. What if they aren't compatible in bed?"

"Exactly," Jake said. "Maybe we need to have one of those—what do you call them—interventions. We'll sit them both down and make sure they know what they're getting into and encourage them to do it."

"But we can't really speak with any authority," Caley said. "Neither one of us has been engaged or married so why would they listen to us?"

"And we haven't had sex," Jake said. "At least, not with each other."

"Well, we are older…and wiser. That should count for something."

Jake considered their dilemma. "You know, we grew up in the same household with our siblings. I guess if the sex was great between us, don't you think the sex would be great between Sam and Emma?"

"Are you suggesting we have sex so that we can use our experience to break up Sam and Emma's wedding? What if the sex were great?"

"Oh, it would be great," Jake said. "I know that for a fact."

"How?"

"By the way you touch me. And by the way you react to my touch. It would be great between us. Maybe Sam and Emma have that feeling, too. Maybe that's why they've been saving it."

He reached out and cupped her cheek in his hand, running his thumb over her lower lip. Caley closed her eyes and tipped her head back, waiting for his kiss. He held back, if only to prove a point. She wanted him and all he had to do was touch her to make her desire burn. He bent close and brushed his lips across hers.

"See," he murmured. "I just kiss you and you melt."

Caley smiled as she looked at him, then ran her hand down his chest to his waist. She brushed her knuckles against the zipper of his jeans. "And what about you?" she asked. "I just touch you and you do the opposite."

Jake groaned. "All I've been thinking about since last night is getting you back in my bed. If I thought I'd have to wait another day to touch you again, I think I'd cut a hole in the ice and jump in the lake."

"Don't do that," Caley teased. "That water is cold and the shrinkage would be horrible."

He laughed, the sound echoing off the trees. "The way you talk. Do you talk to the other men in your life like this?"

"Right now, you're the only man in my life. And it's easy to talk to you." She paused. "You're my oldest friend, Jake. I can say anything to you." She drew a deep breath. "I guess I didn't realize that until now. We haven't seen each other in eleven years and it seems as if nothing's changed. And yet everything has."

"I know," he said. "But it's not all bad." He kissed her again. "So we're okay. About last night?"

"I didn't sleep at all." Caley leaned back against the hood of the car.

"I didn't, either. I'm starting to think we'd do a lot better if we slept together." Jake rested his hands on her waist and stared down into her eyes. "You know you can't live without me."

"I know I can't get my car out of the snow without you," she countered.

He stepped back and carefully examined the task at hand. But the sound of an approaching car caught their attention and Jake watched as an SUV with police lights stopped on the opposite side of the road. The policeman jumped out of the truck and strolled across the road.

"I thought that was you," he said. "What's up, Caley?"

"Hey, Jeff," Caley called, giving the cop a friendly wave.

"If you tell me this happened while you were

talking on your cell phone, you know I'm going to have to arrest you."

"I'm not used to the snow. I skidded on the curve and next thing I knew, I was in the snowbank."

"I've got a tow chain in the truck. I'll pull you out."

Jake watched as Caley gave the guy a dazzling smile. "Could you?" she asked. "That would really be great."

"I'm here to serve," he said with a crooked grin. He looked over at Jake and nodded. "Hey, buddy, you can be on your way. I'll help the lady with her problem."

Caley turned to Jake. "Well, that saves us both some time. Aren't we lucky he came along?"

Jake felt a surge of jealousy course through his body. The reaction stunned him. He remembered feeling that way when they'd been younger, when she'd turned her eyes toward other boys. But Jake had assumed he'd outgrown that particular emotion. "You know each other?"

"That's Jeff Winslow. You remember him. He used to work at the marina. He lived in town. He's the police chief now."

"That's Jeff Winslow?" As a teenager, Winslow considered himself the Casanova of the precollege crowd. He had girls falling at his feet and, according to rumor, he usually picked them up, seduced them and then tossed them aside for new conquests. The guys used to tease him that he'd have to take a second job in order to pay for the condoms he used. "Yeah, I remember him."

"He stopped me the night I got into town. I was talking on my cell phone. He let me off with a warning."

"You can't go out with him," Jake said.

Caley gasped. "He hasn't asked me out."

"He's planning to. I can tell by the look in his eyes. And you can't go out with him. He's a player."

"You know, you used to tell me who I could and couldn't date when we were kids and I used to listen to you," Caley said. "But I'm a big girl now and I can run my own life."

"That's because you were too naive to see what guys really wanted."

"It's no wonder that I remained a virgin until I got to college. I was seriously beginning to develop a complex." She paused. "And I know exactly what *you* want. So see, I have learned a few things." Caley shook her head. "One moment, you're trying to talk me into bed and the next, you're acting like my big brother. No wonder I'm so mixed up."

"I don't want to be your big brother," Jake said.

"Then stop telling me how to run my life."

God, she could be so stubborn at times. Was she this way with all men or was it just him? "Well, I guess you don't need me or my advice. Officer Jeff can take care of all your needs. Automotive and otherwise."

Caley stared at him. "What is this? Are you jealous?"

The accusation stung, even though it was true. Jake trudged back up to the road and Caley trailed after him, stumbling in the deep drift that the plows had pushed aside. He grabbed her waist and helped her through the snow, then brushed off her pant legs when she reached the pavement. "I gotta go try on my tux. I'll see you later. Good luck with Emma."

"Jake, I—"

"I'll talk to you later," he repeated. He strode back to his truck and hopped inside, then skidded out on the road, heading towards town. There were moments when he wondered what he found so fascinating about Caley Lambert. She seemed to go out of her way to exasperate him. If she thought for even a moment that he was dictating to her, she'd dig in her heels and refuse to move.

No, he didn't want to act like her older brother! He had far more carnal interests than that. He looked at her as a woman, a beautiful, sexy, desirable woman. And he wanted her to see him as a man, not that guy who used to drive her crazy every summer.

How could he alter the dynamic of a relationship that seemed as if it were carved in stone? How could he make her see that they'd be so good together? He didn't want her to forget the past. That's what made things so easy between them. He just wanted her to see that they weren't kids anymore.

Things had changed. He'd changed. And he was ready to give her all she'd wanted all those years ago. Only this time, he could give her more than just one night of clumsy lovemaking and empty promises. This time, it could be a beginning.

"WHERE'S HE GOING in such a hurry?"

Caley stared at Jake's truck as it roared off down the snow-covered road. "He has an appointment in town," she murmured.

Jeff watched as he drove off, frowning. "He's speeding. Too fast for conditions. He's lucky I don't chase after him and slap him with a ticket." He walked around to the back of the car and hooked the chain to a metal plate beneath the back bumper. "So, are you and him—"

"Together? No," Caley said. "We're just…old friends."

"You know, he once threatened to beat the crap out of me if I did more than kiss you on our date."

"I guess you weren't too scared of him."

Jeff grinned. "Hey, I knew why you went out with me. It wasn't too hard to see what was going on between you two. He made things pretty clear."

"No," Caley said. "There was never anything. He was just…like an older brother."

"I don't think so," Jeff said as he walked back to his truck. "I'm pretty sure the guy was in love with you."

Caley stepped out onto the road, puzzled by Jeff's revelation. How could he have gotten all that from a simple warning? Still, Jake had admitted as much, only she thought he'd been teasing. What if it was true? What if his feelings had run much deeper than she ever suspected?

Jeff hooked the chain to his truck. He slowly pulled it taut. A moment later, her car began to move as it was gradually drawn back onto the road. "That's good!" she shouted.

Jeff parked the truck. He walked to the front of her rental car and examined it. "No damage," he said.

"Thanks." Caley reached for the door and Jeff quickly opened it for her. "I'm lucky you came along."

"Hey, there's a good band playing out at Tyler's tomorrow night. We could catch some dinner and then head out there. I mean, if you aren't busy with family stuff. And I promise I won't try any funny business."

Caley hesitated. There was absolutely no spark between her and Jeff, and she didn't want to lead him on. Besides, if she wanted sparks, she had the Fourth of July fireworks in Jake. "I'm trying to spend some time with my sister."

"Yeah, I heard she was getting married. Your mom told me when I saw her in town yesterday. That's a surprise. Little Emma Lambert and Sam Burton. Hard to believe they're old enough to get married."

"Maybe Emma and I will stop by and check it out," she said. A girl's night out might make her sister reconsider getting married. She had far too many oats to sow yet and Tyler's Roadhouse was known as a single girl's paradise.

"Well, then, I'll see you if I see you. I know the guy at the door. Just give him your name and he'll let you in without the cover charge. You drive careful now, Caley. I don't want to catch you in another snowbank. If I do, I might have to toss you in jail."

He opened her car door for her and she got inside. As Caley drove off, she glanced in the rearview mirror. Jeff Winslow was an attractive guy. And now that she was single again, she ought to have been flattered that he'd turned his attention to her.

Caley had never put much stock in sexual chemistry, but now she finally understood what it was all about. When she and Jeff sat in the same test tube, nothing happened. But when she got mixed up in a beaker of Jake, the combination erupted into heat and passion and uncontrolled need.

There was a strange connection between them, but she couldn't put her finger on what it was. Something was drawing them together, a power that was impossible to resist. And with every moment that passed, Caley wondered why she even bothered to try.

Her phone rang and Caley reached to get it out of her purse. But then she drew her hand away. For the first time in her professional life, she didn't want to think about work. She didn't want to answer some silly question or explain some figures on a report. She just wanted to be left alone for a day. Grabbing the phone, she switched it off, the Mozart tune ending prematurely. She'd deal with work later. And besides, the last thing she needed was a ticket courtesy of Jeff. She had more important things on her mind.

Her thoughts returned to Jake. There was one major fear holding her back, a fear that she would repeat past mistakes. What if they did have sex and what if it was the most wonderful experience of her life? And what if she fell in love with Jake all over again?

Those feelings had been buried so deep for so long that she'd thought they were gone. But the moment he'd kissed her, they'd floated back to the surface. Caley was much stronger now, but Jake had the capacity to sweep her off her feet, to make her lose touch with reality and reason.

She drew a ragged breath. Though it was frightening, this power he had over her, it was also liberating. When she was with him, she could let go and enjoy herself. For the first time since she was a teenager, she looked forward to getting up in the morning. While she was here with Jake, she didn't have to worry about all the public relations fires she'd have to put out in the course of a day, all the upset clients and curious reporters and skittish stockholders. She could relax and just be herself.

Why was it that Jake was always a factor in the choices she made? She'd gone to school at NYU because she thought it would impress Jake. She got a job in public relations because Jake had once told her she was good at solving problems. She'd worked herself ragged in the past seven years because, deep inside, she wanted to prove that she didn't need Jake in her life to be happy.

And where had it gotten her? Caley sighed softly. Right back to where she started, still chasing after Jake Burton. But this time, he was chasing after her, as well. And she now had control over what happened between them—until, of course, he touched her. Then all bets were off.

"That's the problem," Caley said. "I can control my attraction for Jake as long as we aren't close to each other. But I'm so attracted to him, I can't stay away. I'm damned if I do and damned if I don't."

BY THE TIME she got back to the inn it was nearly noon.

There was no one at the desk when she walked in, but Caley found her younger sister at a table in the dining room, a binder open in front of her. She munched on a breadstick as she flipped through the pages.

"Your maid of honor has arrived," Caley said, pulling out a chair across from Emma.

Her sister looked up and smiled. "Good. I need someone to distract me from all these details. My mind is so filled with minutiae that it's starting to leak out of my ears. Flowers, music, candles, dinner. I thought we were planning a small wedding, but it's starting to take on a life of its own."

Caley sat down, then reached out for the binder, scanning down her sister's "to do" list. She didn't understand why brides worried over such silly decisions. "This is the list of music? Go for the Pachelbel's "Canon" for the processional and "Ode to Joy" for the recessional. Red roses with my bridesmaid's dress would be too much. White would be better. And not the hybrid roses but the cabbage roses. Vanilla-scented tapers for the candles—you know how much Mom loves those. And surf and turf for dinner, that way you'll please everyone." Caley slammed the binder shut. "There, that was easy."

Emma blinked in surprise. "Caroline Lenore Lambert! You can't just decide so quickly. All of these things have to be discussed."

"With whom? Sam? He doesn't care. I've heard that brides often focus so much time and attention on the wedding that they forget there's a marriage that comes after it."

"That's why we wanted to keep this small," Emma

said. "And more manageable. Between Mom and Mrs. Burton, we wouldn't have had a wedding, we would have had an event. But I don't want to make decisions just to get them out of the way. I want this wedding to be perfect. So does Sam."

"So you have to discuss everything with him?"

"No. He's leaving the details up to me."

Caley plucked a breadstick out of the basket and munched on the end. "That's odd. I mean, that he wouldn't even care. You know how those Burton boys are. They're so bossy. They have to run everything."

Caley could see Emma growing dizzy from the change in conversation. Tiny worry lines furrowed her brow and she kept glancing back down at her book, as if all the answers were contained within.

Caley couldn't help but feel a little guilty, but this marriage would be a life-altering event and if Emma wasn't prepared then Caley wasn't doing her job as a big sister or a maid of honor. "If it isn't perfect then the marriage will never succeed. It's like bad karma."

Emma frowned. "Yeah. I guess so." She paused. "Is it? Is that some superstition I haven't heard yet?"

"You're marrying the perfect guy so you have to be perfect in return. So did you solve your motorcycle dilemma? I'd stand firm on that one. Once you give in, he's going to take advantage and think he can run the show."

"He doesn't want to talk about it. He says it's his decision."

"Emma, things will only get worse after you're married. Marriage magnifies problems, it doesn't make them go away." It was armchair psychology and a deliberate manipulation but if it saved Emma from making the biggest mistake of her life, then Caley didn't care. If love couldn't withstand a bit of poking and prodding, then it would never last.

Caley winced inwardly. It almost pained her to say those words. But maybe that's why she wasn't happily married and living in the suburbs with 2.5 kids. Perhaps there was some truth in what she said. She reached out and took Emma's hand. "Are you really ready for this, Em?"

"I-I've thought about postponing," Emma admitted in a small voice. "But then, I just wrote it off to nerves. Everyone would be so disappointed."

"This is about you, not Mom and Dad," Caley said.

"But how am I supposed to know for sure? What am I supposed to feel?"

"Passion, contentment, anticipation. You're going to spend the rest of your life with this one man. You have to know that when you look at him over the breakfast table in thirty years, that he was and is the only man in the world for you." Caley sat back in her chair. "If you called it off, Emma, I would stand behind you. I'd help you explain it to Mom and Dad."

Emma drew a shaky breath and then forced a bright smile. "That's what you do for a living, right? Take disasters and put a pretty ribbon on them and pretend they never happened?"

"This wouldn't be a disaster," Caley insisted. But a divorce in two or three years would be. The families would be forced to take sides and that would destroy the lifelong friendship that they'd all enjoyed.

Emma shook her head. "Don't be silly. I'm not going to call it off. It's just prewedding jitters, that's all." She grabbed a menu from the center of the table and handed it to Caley. "Here. Why don't you order something for lunch. I'm going to run up to my room and get the folder from the florist and we'll discuss the bouquets. The florist needs to know by this afternoon so he can place the order."

Emma pushed back from the table and hurried out of the dining room. Caley slowly shook her head. The doubts she had before hadn't been dispelled. If anything, they were now magnified. Emma wasn't ready to get married, but she also wasn't strong enough to make the decision on her own. If the wedding were going to be called off, then Jake would have to talk Sam into doing it.

Caley grabbed Emma's binder and opened it again. It was filled with pictures torn from magazines and neatly scribbled notes. There was a whole section on bridesmaid's dresses and another on bridal gowns. It was obvious that Emma had been planning for this wedding for much longer than a month and a half. Some of the photos were at least five years old.

Caley groaned inwardly. Did Emma feel the same way about Sam as Caley had felt about Jake? Had she carried a secret crush around all these years? If she had, then trying to convince Emma to wait was going to be a much tougher job than she anticipated.

Motioning to the waitress, Caley stood up. "Can you let my sister know that I had to run an errand? I'll be back later this afternoon."

If she and Jake expected to have any effect at all, then they'd better coordinate their efforts. She reached for her cell phone before she realized she wasn't even sure Jake had a cell phone. How did a person exist in this world without one? Or without wireless computer access and a PDA and a fax machine?

Caley strode to her car, then remembered that Jake had an appointment to try on his tuxedo. The only place in town that rented men's formal wear was a shop two blocks down and around the corner. Caley glanced over at her car parked in front of the inn and decided it would be faster to walk.

When she arrived, she was out of breath. She walked to the rear of the store and the small section devoted to formal wear. An elderly man with a tape measure around his neck stood in front of a mirror. "Is Jake Burton here?" she asked.

"He's changing," the man said, pointing to a nearby fitting room. "He'll be out in a moment."

Caley strode over to the fitting room door, opened it and stepped inside. Jake stood in front of the mirror in his boxers and a formal shirt. He saw her reflection and smiled.

"You have a perfectly nice room at the inn and I'm staying out in the boathouse. Why do we keep meeting in fitting rooms?"

"We have to talk," Caley said. He slowly turned and her breath caught in her throat. His muscular chest was visible, his shirt half unbuttoned, and Caley's fingers twitched as she imagined the feel of his skin beneath her hands.

Jake reached out and grabbed her wrist, then placed her palm on his chest. "So what is so important that it can't wait until I'm dressed?" He dragged her hand over his chest to his belly, then left it resting near the waistband of his boxers.

She traced her thumb along the deep cut of muscle that ran along his hip to somewhere beneath the blue-striped fabric. Caley wanted to follow it farther, to explore his body until she knew every plane and angle and curve and indentation. His body was flawless, a perfect specimen of male beauty.

She'd never paid much attention to physical

beauty before, but then she'd never been with a truly beautiful man until now. Now, every detail, from the hard muscle of Jake's abdomen to the soft dusting of hair across his chest, intrigued her.

She ran her hands back over his chest, watching as his growing erection pressed against the front of his boxers. He pulled her toward him and kissed her, cupping her backside in his hands and moving his hips against her. Emboldened, Caley reached down and wrapped her fingers around his shaft, hot and hard through the soft fabric.

Jake's breath caught and then he moaned. "What are you doing?"

"I'm not sure," Caley said. And she wasn't. She was just following her instincts. It didn't make any sense and in the rational world, she might have been appalled at her daring. But when she and Jake were together, the normal rules didn't seem to apply.

"How does it fit?" the salesclerk called.

"It fits good," Jake replied, his eyes closed, his face a mask of pleasure. He wasn't talking about the clothes. They fit—her hand, his shaft, his hands, her backside. Everything seemed to fit perfectly.

"Can I see?"

"No!" they both said.

Jake looked down at her through passion-glazed eyes and smiled. "Is that why you came here? To torment me?"

"I—I came to talk about Emma," she admitted, realizing how far off track she'd wandered. She hesitantly drew her hand away.

"Don't," he whispered. "Touch me." Jake brushed his lips across hers. "I'm sorry I acted like such an ass earlier. I was out of line. Do you forgive me?"

"For what?"

"For what I said. For the way I acted. For being a jerk and leaving you out on the road with Winslow." He sucked in a sharp breath and moaned. "If you keep doing that, there will be consequences. Very messy consequences."

"Sorry," Caley said. "Maybe we should continue this later?"

"Maybe that would be best," he said. "I'm not sure I want our first time to be in a fitting room." He glanced down. "This is definitely going to affect the fit of my trousers."

Caley giggled. She sensed that sex with Jake would be amazing, heart-stopping, a powerful experience. But she also knew that it would be fun. And Caley had never really had a lot of fun in the bedroom. Sex had always been fraught with so many expectations, many of them never fulfilled. She was curious now, anxious to learn how it might be with Jake. "Maybe I should leave?"

"No, just give me a few minutes. I just have to focus on something else."

"Our plan," she said. "We need a plan. I talked to Emma and she's having doubts. I don't think she's ready, but she won't be the one to call it off."

Jake glanced around. "You know, this fitting room thing is pretty hot. It's like a public place but it's still private."

Caley gave him a soft punch on the arm. "We're talking about Emma and Sam."

"I don't want to talk about them. I'd rather talk about us. What are you doing this afternoon? I have something to show you."

Caley looked down, then rolled her eyes. "All you think about is sex."

"No. That's not true. And that's not what I was planning to show you." He grabbed her shoulders and turned her around. "Let me take care of this first." He opened the fitting room door and pushed her out.

The salesclerk was standing outside, a disapproving scowl on his face. "He'll be right out. I'm just going to wait up front. You have some very nice leather chairs." She forced a smile, but the man's expression didn't waver.

Ten minutes later, Jake joined her at the front of the store. He took her hand and walked out with her and when they reached the street, Caley turned on him. "You have to stop making me do those things," she said.

"You used to be such a daredevil," he said. "What's happened?"

"I've grown up," Caley said.

"I dare you to kiss me, right here," Jake said. "In front of everyone." He looked around at the nearly empty street and then shrugged. "All right, in front of that woman with the poodle."

"Where are we going? You said you wanted to take me somewhere."

"I don't know if I should," Jake teased. "You've lost your nerve. I'm not sure this Caley would be up for what I have in mind."

She grinned, then threw her arms around his neck and kissed him deeply. Her tongue slipped between his lips and Caley used every ounce of her feminine wiles to arouse him again. "I'm just a little out of practice," she said. "The only daring thing I do is dodging cabs when crossing Fifth Avenue."

Jake grabbed another kiss, then pulled her along to his SUV. Caley really didn't care where they were going, as long as it was somewhere quiet and private where they might continue what they'd started in the fitting room.

4

"WHERE ARE WE GOING?"

Jake glanced over at Caley and smiled.

After their rocky start that morning, Jake wondered whether he and Caley were doomed to spend their time revisiting the past.

They'd been such good friends growing up, doing everything together, climbing trees and exploring the lakeshore, fishing and swimming. But once they'd started to see each other as more than just good buddies, their relationship had grown strained. Though they'd still spent the majority of their time together, they had often been locked in a battle of wills, each of them trying to one-up the other.

Caley had used the stubborn determination he'd fostered and made a success of herself in a highly competitive field. He, in turn, had internalized her absolute confidence in him and used it to build his own business from scratch.

He'd never really thanked her for being such a

good friend. But he didn't want to do that now. Instead, he wanted her to look at him as something more than a friend. He wanted to get back to that place, to that day right before they'd started looking at each other with teenage lust in their eyes. If he took them back, then maybe they'd be able to turn things in a different direction.

"I'd just like to know what this thing you're going to show me is."

"A surprise," Jake said. "Are you always this impatient? Or do you just hate surprises?"

"Both," Caley said.

"You're going to have to relax. You're not in the big city anymore. Take a breath, chill for a while. Enjoy the beautiful day."

Caley's phone rang and she pulled it out of her pocket, but before she could answer it, Jake grabbed it from her hands. "You can talk to them later," he said, taking a quick glance at the caller ID.

"I have responsibilities," Caley said. She took her cell phone back. "Don't you have a cell phone? Don't people from your office need to talk to you?"

"They don't have my number. I don't want anyone calling me so I don't give it out. When I leave the office, I'm done. Whatever they need can wait or they can figure it out for themselves. I'm not that important that I have all the answers. Are you?"

Caley frowned as if perplexed by his question.

"Well, yes. That's how you get to be the boss. By having all the answers."

"Maybe you should trust the people you work with a little more. If you don't, you'll drive yourself crazy."

Jake knew from experience that it was best to take a more relaxed approach to work. When he first opened his own architectural firm in Chicago, he'd spent months of sleepless nights worrying about all the horrible things that might befall him professionally. And then, once he was sure they weren't going to come and repossess the office furniture, he stopped worrying. He didn't want to be a millionaire or appear on the cover of some glossy architecture magazine. He wasn't going to be the next I. M. Pei. He'd do his job well, he'd make a decent living and his clients would be happy with his work. That was enough.

"I work better when I'm crazy," Caley said. She flipped open the phone. "Give me your number. I might have an emergency sometime."

"I'll only give you my number if you promise that you'll use it," he said.

"For what? A booty call?"

"Maybe. Or a little bit of drunk dialing. Or when you get stuck in a snowbank on the side of the road." He reached in his jacket pocket and pulled out his own phone, then handed it to her. "Put your number on my memory dial. I might have an emergency of my own some night."

Jake carefully watched the side of the East Shore Road, looking for the weathered wooden sign that hung from an old maple tree. Havenwoods. When he saw it, he turned sharply into the woods, steering the truck down a snow-covered drive.

Caley looked around. "What is this? It said private property on that sign. We shouldn't drive down here."

"Relax," Jake said. "The owner hardly ever uses it in the winter. No one has been here for a while." Caley was silent and Jake looked over at her. "It'll be all right, I promise."

They wound through the woods and finally came to a clearing in the trees. An old log house stood on the rise above the lake. A ramshackle porch, supported by a stone foundation, surrounded the house and three fieldstone chimneys broke up the roofline. Every time Jake saw it, he couldn't help but be amazed that it was finally his.

"Oh my God," Caley murmured, peering through the windshield. "It's the Fortress." She glanced over at Jake, a wide smile on her face. "I haven't been here in…years. It still looks exactly the same." She frowned. "But smaller."

"It's called Havenwoods," Jake said, "and I found out it was one of the first summerhouses built on this lake, back when the industrialists called their summer homes camps and North Lake was just a pretty fishing hole in the middle of a forest. It was built in 1885 by a railroad tycoon from Chicago who owned the entire lake and the surrounding property. It was designed by William West Durant," Jake continued. "Durant was the first to design in the Great Camp style in the Adirondacks."

"Someone is home," she said. "The porch lights are on in the middle of the day."

He shook his head. "The lighting is triggered by a sensor on the driveway. When you come from the lake side, the lights don't go on." He turned off the car. "You want to go inside?"

As kids, they used to come across the lake by boat and tie up at the rotting dock. They'd explored every inch of the property and had spent many rainy days inside the house, gaining entrance through a first-floor window with a broken sash lock.

"We can't go inside. That's trespassing. And breaking and entering."

"We used to do it all the time. No one will care," Jake said. "And I know where the key is so we won't have to break in." He jumped out of the truck and circled around, then helped her out. "If Officer Winslow catches us, you can just smile at him and he won't arrest us."

Caley's gaze was fixed on the facade as she walked closer. "You brought me here on my fifteenth birthday. And you gave me that arrowhead necklace.

I wore that thing all year. My girlfriends in school thought it was the ugliest thing, but I thought…well, I thought it was special."

"Do you still have it?"

"I do. It's in my closet back in New York. The leather string broke, but I kept it. Along with everything else you gave me." Caley smiled. "I'll have to get that box and go through it."

"What else is in it?"

"Silly stuff. Mementos of our grand love affair. There's a piece of bubblegum you gave me. I was sure it meant that you wanted me. I used to take it out and touch it because I knew it had been in your pocket."

"That's a little scary," Jake teased.

"I know. I was a teenage girl hauling around a huge torch. Everything meant something."

They climbed the snow-covered steps and Caley walked to the window, peering inside, her hands around her eyes. "It looks the same. I'd imagine this was a beautiful place to visit in its day."

Jake walked along the outside wall until he reached the second set of windows, then bent down and pulled a stone from a spot beneath the sill. Beneath it, he found the keys.

"How did you know about that?"

"I was here alone one summer and the caretaker showed up. I saw him get the keys. After that, I could get in whenever I wanted." He grinned and grabbed Caley's hand and pulled her along to the corner of the house. "See this. These logs were hand-notched so they fit really tight. Durant always used materials from the surrounding forest."

Jake unlocked the three locks on the front door, then opened it. He stepped aside, waiting for Caley to enter. "It'll be all right. I promise."

They stood in the entry hall, an old deer-antler chandelier hanging above their head. The furniture was tattered and dusty, but he'd managed to clean up most of the mess left by the leaky roof and broken windows.

"Wow," Caley said. "This place needs a lot of work. It seemed like a palace when we were kids, but now I see it for what it is."

"Look beyond the surface," Jake said. "Can you see what it could be again?"

"I can," she said. She walked over to a low bench made of branches and twigs. "But it would take someone with a lot of time and a lot of money."

"I used to walk through this house and memorize all the details. This is why I decided to become an architect. I wanted to design houses like this. Summerhouses. Places where people relax and have fun."

Jake felt her take his hand and weave her fingers through his. It was a simple gesture, but he instantly knew she understood. He wasn't sure anyone else would. But Caley would. It seemed right that he share this with her again. "Come on, I'll show you around."

Though he hadn't kissed her or even touched her in an intimate way, Jake felt as though they'd suddenly become so much closer. This was who he was now, not the boy she'd known. And the woman standing beside him understood what it all meant.

They wandered aimlessly, Caley taking in all the details silently, as if caught in her memories of the past. Dust motes swirled around them in the light that filtered through the windows. When they passed through a shaft of sunlight, Jake gently pulled her into his arms and kissed her, his mouth searching for a familiar taste he'd come to crave.

"I need you," he murmured, his lips warm against hers.

Caley looked up at him, her gaze fixed on his mouth. "Show me the rest of the house," she murmured.

They walked slowly through each of the six bedrooms, Jake pointing out the architectural details that made Havenwoods so special. By the time they got back to the entry hall, Jake was almost desperate to kiss her. But he waited, hoping that this place would work its magic.

It was a great wreck of a house, but it was part of their history together, part of who he'd become. It deserved better than to be consumed by the elements and left for some errant campfire spark to take hold of and burn down.

He'd mortgaged his future to buy it, cashing in his investments, selling his sports car to buy a second-hand SUV. He'd even sold his house in Wicker Park and took up residence in a tiny one-bedroom in a seedy neighborhood, just so he could afford the mortgage and taxes.

It left little for renovations, but Jake felt it was worth the risk. Although, he still hadn't told a soul he owned it. His father would probably blow a gasket and his mother would never understand. But he had an ally in Caley.

"There are only two things I ever really wanted in my life. And this was one of them," Jake said.

"What was the other?" Caley asked.

"You," he said with a devilish grin.

JAKE LOCKED THE FRONT DOOR behind them and returned the key to its spot beneath the window. Caley watched him, her mind flooded with memories of their childhood. She couldn't count the number of days they'd spent at the Fortress. It had been a magical place, a place all their own.

It was sweet of him to remember, she mused. Even when things had been difficult between them, Caley had been able to count on Jake. As teenagers, they'd argue and pout, but he'd always be the first to come back with an apology—a gift of something he'd found in the forest or a plan for a brand-new adventure or just a silly joke that would make her laugh.

It wasn't difficult to understand why she'd been in love with him all those years ago. When she was with him, she felt as if she were the most important person in his world. And she felt that way now. There was an honesty between them, a respect that she'd never felt with any other man.

When he stepped back to her side, she wrapped her arms around his waist and pushed up on her toes, dropping a soft kiss on his lips. "Thank you," she said.

"For what?"

"For bringing me back here."

Jake slipped his hands around her waist and drew her closer, his mouth covering hers. The kiss was quiet and gentle, his tongue caressing hers in a slow, seductive way.

It was as if they both finally knew that being together was inevitable. There was nothing stopping them anymore. All day she'd been thinking about this, about what even one kiss would do to her. If a kiss could devastate her defenses so easily, what would a night in bed do?

Suddenly, Caley wanted to find out. She didn't need to weigh the consequences of what she was about to do because she didn't care anymore about consequences. All she cared about was sharing herself, completely, with Jake.

"Would you like go back to the inn?" she asked.

"I thought we could walk down to the lake," Jake said. "There's something else I want to show you."

"I want to go back to the inn," Caley said. "With you."

He stared down into her eyes, an odd expression on his face. Then a slow smile curved the corners of his mouth. "We don't have to go back there," he murmured.

"We don't?"

He pulled her along the porch, circling the house until he'd reached the side that faced the lake. She saw the small log building about thirty yards from the house, connected by a covered walkway. They'd called it the Guardhouse when they were kids, but now Caley knew what it really was—a summer kitchen. When they reached the front door, Jake pulled out his keys and unlocked the padlock.

"You have your own key?" she asked.

Jake opened the door. "Yeah. It comes in handy since I own the place," he murmured.

Caley gasped, not sure that she heard him right. "You own this cabin?"

"No, I own the whole thing. The house, the property, the rotting dock and the roofless guest cabins. The musty furniture and that old moose head over the fireplace. It's all mine."

Caley glanced around the small cabin. A drafting table was set up near the window and a small cot stood in front of the fireplace. She walked over to the table and stared down at the yellowed plans spread out there, recognizing the facade of the main house. They were covered with yellow sticky notes in Jake's handwriting.

Caley felt her heart warm, suddenly understanding the deeper reasons for their visit. This was his home. And he wanted her approval. "I can't believe this is all yours," she said. "How did you get it?"

"I was in New York for a seminar and I decided to look up the lady who owned it. I had the name from the tax records. We had tea and I told her about how much I loved the place and how I used to sneak in here. And she agreed to sell it to me, with the provision that I bring it back to what it was in her childhood. I made a promise and I intend to keep it. And when it's finished, she asked that I invite her grandchildren to stay now and then."

"Why did you bring me here?"

"It's our place," Jake said. "I thought you should see it again. Because you're my oldest friend and you'd appreciate it."

Caley slowly unzipped her jacket. "I don't want

to be your friend right now," she said, dropping the jacket on the rough plank floor.

He reached out and rubbed her arms through her shirt. "Maybe I should start a fire."

Caley sat on the edge of the cot and watched as he crumpled newspapers up beneath the grate in the old stone hearth. He tossed some smaller logs on top, then grabbed a match and started the fire. They both stared into the flames as they licked at the dry logs. Soon, a gentle heat was radiating through the room.

"Do you stay here often?" she asked.

"When I come out from the city," Jake said. "It's harder in the summer since my folks are in town. Then, I have to stay with them. In the winter, no one knows I'm here. I work on the house. It's quiet and I get some of my other work done, too."

"I'm used to having so many people around," she said. "I can't imagine getting anything done with all this silence."

"Sometimes silence is nice," he said, leaning forward to kiss her.

She reached for the buttons of her shirt, and Jake drew a ragged breath. Pressing her hand to his chest, she felt his heart pounding beneath her fingers. Caley was breathless, as if the anticipation itself was exhausting.

"Are you sure you want to do this here?" he asked. "Conditions are a little rough."

"This is perfect," Caley said. In truth, she'd always dreamed that it would happen this way with Jake, in some secret spot where no one would ever find them, in the back seat of his beat-up Cutlass or on a secluded beach in the middle of the night.

Jake reached into his jeans pocket and pulled out his wallet, then retrieved a condom. "I guess we'll need this," he said.

"Are you nervous?" Caley asked, reaching out to grab the front of his jacket and pull him down on top of her.

"No," he said with a grin. "Well, maybe a little. God, I feel as if we're in high school and this is my first time."

"I know. Me, too." She tugged on his jacket, drawing it down over his arms, then tossing it aside. "It makes it more exciting, don't you think?"

Caley got up on her knees and shoved her shirt off her arms, dropping it on top of his jacket. Jake rubbed his thumb over her nipple, bringing it to a peak beneath the silky fabric of her bra. "Sweetheart, getting naked with you would be just as exciting if we did it in the middle of Main Street with all of North Lake watching."

They tugged and tore at each other's clothes, their hands frantically skimming over each inch of naked skin. The air was still chilly and his touch raised goose bumps. But it only made each sensation more acute, exciting her so much that she trembled with each caress. Caley felt alive with anticipation, scared and nervous and aroused all at once.

When they were both down to their underwear, they stopped and stared at each other. Caley giggled softly. "Now what?"

"I'm the virgin here," Jake teased. "Maybe you should show me what to do."

Caley reached out and ran her finger over his lower lip. He was giving her control, letting her set the pace. This time, she would seduce him, like she'd tried to do all those years ago. And this time, she'd succeed.

She slid her hands along his body and hooked her fingers in the waistband of his boxers, then pulled them down. After that, she quickly took care of her own underwear. His body radiated heat, more than the fire burning on the hearth. He pulled her against him and his warmth became hers.

Stretched out on top of him, Caley reveled in the feel of their naked bodies pressed against each other. He ran his hands over her back, along her hips. She could feel his desire, hot and hard, between them.

She'd wanted to take everything slowly, to savor each moment. But she was impatient, desperate to experience it all at once. She'd waited for so long and now that she'd made the decision to have him, there would be nothing stopping her. She drew back, pressing a line of kisses to his chest, moving lower and lower until she reached the soft hair on his belly.

Caley knew the power of his touch on her body. Now, she wanted to test her power over him. She stroked him, wrapping her fingers around his hard shaft. Jake closed his eyes and groaned, his breath coming his short gasps. He arched into her touch and when she looked up again, his eyes were open and he was watching her every move.

"I don't think my first time felt this good."

Caley smiled, then dipped lower and took him into her mouth. Her touch was like shock to his body and he jerked, sucking in a sharp breath. "Am I doing it right?" she teased, smiling up at him.

"Oh, yeah. Oh, that's so nice."

Caley continued to caress him with her tongue and her lips, carefully gauging his reaction and drawing him away from the edge again and again. And when she suspected that he wouldn't last much longer, she moved back up along his body, until his swollen shaft rested between her legs.

She rocked above him, his erection sliding against her sex, the friction sending wonderful waves of pleasure through her body. In the past, sex had always been filled with nagging disappointments. She'd never really felt the kind of passion that she'd wanted to feel, that she knew she could feel.

This time, it would be different. Caley felt as if she

could surrender by simply closing her eyes and letting herself go. She was so close already and he hadn't even touched her. An urgency drove her forward, toward something that she'd never experienced yet knew she wanted. Caley reached out and took the condom from Jake's hand, then unwrapped it.

"Wait," he murmured. "Slow down."

"I've been waiting eleven years," she said. "I can't wait any longer." She sheathed him, then straddled his hips, moving above him until he probed at her entrance. Then, with a deep sigh, she sank down on top of him.

The sensation of him filling her was a revelation. It was perfection and paradise, absolute intimacy. They were closer than they'd ever been before and yet it seemed so natural, as if their bodies had been made for this all along.

Jake began to move inside her, his gaze fixed on hers, his fingers tangled in hers. Caley leaned forward and ran her tongue along the crease of his mouth. He reached out and drew her into a deep, desperate kiss, his lips and tongue communicating his need without words.

This was sex, but it was more than that, Caley thought to herself. It was passion and instinct, a need that had burned inside them for years. It was the past and the present, it was the two of them drowning in a world of pleasure. Now she understood why it hadn't happened all those years ago. She wasn't ready—they weren't ready—for the intensity of their joining.

Jake reached between them to touch her, but Caley grabbed his hand again and pinned it at his side. She was already just a heartbeat away and his touch would send her over. Instead, she increased her tempo, rocking faster and faster and feeling the tension tighten inside her. She ached to let go, but knew that if she waited just a bit longer, it would be all the more intense. She wanted to come, but she wanted it to be the most powerful release she'd ever experienced.

Jake wasn't content to play a passive role anymore. He sat up and wrapped her legs around his waist, impaling her until she could feel him deep inside her. When he began to move again, she knew she was lost. Every stroke was exquisite torture.

Caley felt herself reaching for ecstasy, her release so close she could almost touch it. And then it came down on her like a waterfall, washing over her until her whole body tingled with sensation. She cried out as spasm after spasm shook her, her body reacting uncontrollably.

And then, suddenly, Jake was there with her, driving into her one last time before joining her. He pressed his face between her breasts as he moaned, his hands clutching at her shoulders, driving her down onto him again and again until he was completely spent.

When their shudders had subsided, they collapsed into each other, Jake gathering her in his arms. It had happened so quickly and yet Caley felt complete and utter exhaustion. Her body, so tense just moments before, was almost boneless. "Oh, my," she murmured.

"Why did we wait so long?" he asked, pressing a kiss beneath her ear.

"It wouldn't have been this good eleven years ago," she said.

"I'm not talking about then. I'm talking about the past two days." He raked his hand through her tangled hair, then gently tugged back until she met his gaze. "This changes everything."

Caley frowned. "It does?"

"How am I supposed to be around you now? How can I keep from touching you and kissing you? I want you in my bed. Tonight. Tomorrow night. For as long as you want me."

"I guess this won't count as a one-night stand?"

"No," Jake said, shaking his head. "I don't think there's a chance of that. You can't resist me."

"And you can't resist me," she countered with a satisfied smile.

"Why should I even try?"

Caley snuggled up against his warm body. "We can stay here tonight. I know the guy who owns the place." She pressed her lips to his chest, then sighed.

"No one is expecting us back," Jake said.

"Except for Emma. But she can wait." Caley pushed up on her elbow and brushed a lock of hair from his forehead. "So we could do it again?"

"Yeah," Jake replied. But then his smile faded and he cursed softly. "No. I only had one condom."

"There are other things we could do," Caley suggested.

"Really? I always loved your sense of adventure," he replied, grabbing her waist and pulling her beneath him.

His mouth came down on hers and Caley lost herself in his kiss. There were a lot things she'd never tried in the bedroom. But with Jake, all her inhibitions seemed to dissolve at his touch. She didn't feel vulnerable with him, she felt powerful. She didn't have to worry about what he wanted or needed because he wanted nothing more than to give her pleasure. She could let go and enjoy his body without sacrificing a part of herself.

They had been friends first and now they were lovers. There would be no going back.

"No, DON'T GO," Jake said, pulling Caley back into his arms. "Not yet. Stay a little longer."

Caley glanced over her shoulder at him, snuggled beneath the covers of his bed in the boathouse. They'd officially been lovers for twenty-four hours and the sneaking around was already wearing thin.

After dinner at the Lamberts', Caley had offered up some silly story about working on their toasts for the wedding. They walked down to the boathouse and the moment the door closed behind them, they were tossing aside clothes and tumbling into Jake's bed.

Jake had spent last night in Caley's bed at the inn, sneaking out in the early morning hours so that he could get back to the boathouse before anyone noticed him missing. They were two adults and yet there were moments when Jake felt as if they were teenagers.

"Don't you think it's odd?"

"What?" Caley asked as she continued to dress.

"What we're doing is perfectly legal. Between consenting adults. And we have a variety of locations to choose from. We shouldn't have to worry about getting caught."

"It would complicate things," Caley explained. "There would be questions and speculation and expectations. I just want this to be about you and me and not our families, all right?"

Jake nodded. "So do you want me to sneak into your bed tonight?"

Caley grabbed her jacket and reached into the pocket, then withdrew a key, dangling it in front of his face. "I got you your own. Just don't let Emma see you come in. She's been going to bed early, so come over as soon as you can get away." She gave him a quick kiss, then pulled her boots on. "Are we agreed on our plan?"

Over the course of the past day, he and Caley had come up with a strategy to test Sam and Emma's commitment to each other. They'd discussed all the pitfalls and problems that couples encountered on the path to everlasting love and had put together an obstacle course for Sam and Emma to navigate. "Operation Wedding Trashers is ready to go."

"We're not trying to trash their wedding," Caley said. "We're just testing the depth of their feelings. Nothing more sinister than what a good marriage counselor would do."

"Except we have absolutely no professional qualifications or practical experience in marital matters."

"No. But we do have relationship experience," Caley said. "That should count for something." She sat down on the edge of the bed, now fully dressed in all her cold-weather clothes. "So tomorrow night I'm going to take Emma to Tyler's with me. There are always lots of single guys there to dance with and I'll make sure she drinks plenty of cocktails."

"And I'm taking Sam out for some fun. There's a strip club out on the interstate. I figured we'd go there."

Caley's eyes went wide. "Really? Is it one of those clubs where they take off all their clothes?"

"Almost," Jake said. "Just G-strings, shiny poles and lots of dollar bills."

"So you've been there before?"

Jake shook his head. "No. But I've heard about it. Brett and a bunch of his college buddies went there for his twenty-first birthday. Does it bother you that I'll be looking at naked women?"

"Of course not," Caley said.

"Because it would bother me if you were out looking at naked men."

"Maybe I should see if I can find a strip club for Emma and me to go to. There has to be one somewhere," Caley said.

"There's only one body I'm interested in seeing naked," Jake said. "And that would be yours. You don't have to worry. After what we've had together, a hundred naked women aren't going to get me excited."

"Good answer," Caley said. She lay down on top of him and gave him a more thorough kiss. "Later."

"I'm counting on it," he said.

She walked to the door, sending him a smile before she slipped out. Jake listened to her footsteps on the stairs. He crawled out of bed, wrapping the comforter around his naked body, then peered through the curtains to watch her run across the lawn toward the Lambert house.

The boathouse was now a cozy little haven. The heater had been running all day and though it was a bit chilly inside, it was comfortable. His mother had given him a down comforter and Brett had turned on the water so the bathroom was functioning. The accommodations were almost perfect, and almost completely private.

Jake flopped back down on the bed and closed his eyes. He'd made love to his fair share of beautiful women and each time he'd searched for that connection, that spark that might prove he'd found the right one. In the past twenty-four hours he'd realized that it was there with Caley. Maybe it had always been there.

But what did that mean? They lived in different worlds, lived different lives. Though he wanted to believe that love would conquer all, Jake certainly knew the realities of a relationship. Caley had made it clear that their affair would end when she went back to New York. Though he planned to do everything in his power to convince her otherwise, Jake had to prepare himself for the probability that it would be over at the end of the week.

He had known it would be difficult before, but now that they'd become lovers, it would be impossible. Surely, it wouldn't be easy for her, either. Her desire for him ran just as deep and Jake sensed that with every touch, every kiss, the bond between them grew stronger.

And if Caley left him, if things between them ended, he didn't think there would ever be another woman to take her place. In the back of his mind he'd always compared the women he met to Caley. He hadn't been aware of that fact until now. They'd been smart, but Caley had been smarter. They'd been beautiful, but she had beauty they'd never possess. He'd grown up wanting her and only her. Now that he'd had her, he was left to deal with the fear of losing her.

Jake threw his arm over his eyes and cursed softly. A knock sounded on the door and he sat up, surprised that she'd returned so quickly. He waited for her to come in, but she knocked again. Jake grabbed his boxers and pulled them on, then crossed the room and opened the door. But Caley wasn't standing outside. Sam was.

His brother peered inside. "Can I come in?"

"Sure," Jake said, stepping back to allow Sam to pass. "What's up? It's late."

Sam began to pace the width of the room, his shoulders tense, his expression grim. Then, he sat down on the edge of the bed and nervously twisted his fingers together. "I did like you told me. When I drove Emma back to the inn tonight, I told her it was time we were honest with each other. I said we needed to have sex before we got married."

"And she refused?"

"No," Sam said. "No, we had sex." He shook his head. "And it was pretty bad."

Jake frowned. "Bad? Like how bad?"

Sam flopped back and covered his face with his hands. "About as bad as it could get. She was so excited and so was I—at first. I wanted it to be romantic and special, but everything I did seemed so forced. And then, I—I couldn't—you know."

"Get it up?"

"More like, keep it up," Sam said. He turned and looked at Jake. "You don't think I need Viagra, do you?"

Jake chuckled softly. "You haven't had any problems before, have you?"

"No! Never. But I was never marrying any of those other girls. What if this is the way it is with Emma? What if I can't...perform?"

"This happens occasionally. To every guy."

"Did it ever happen to you?"

"Well, no. But I was never under the kind of pressure you are. When I encouraged you to have sex with her, I didn't mean that you should do it just to get it done. It's not like mowing the lawn or changing the oil in your car. There's more to it than that."

"Like foreplay," Sam said. "I know, I tried that, but she was in such a hurry. I started out thinking I'd have to convince her, but she was completely on board. I guess Caley told her it was important to be sexually compatible with your husband." Sam paused. "I think Emma said *crucial*. That was the word. Or maybe it was *critical*. And that's when I started to get really nervous."

"Yeah, I can see how that could happen," Jake said.

Still, he couldn't really relate. With Caley, there was a need there that seemed to overwhelm all rational thought. When they were intimate, he didn't worry about the mechanics, it just happened. It was raw, primal instinct that aroused him. And the fact that it always ended with incredible pleasure was nature at work.

Jake sat down beside his brother and patted him on the back. "This doesn't mean it will happen that way every time."

"What if it does? I wouldn't want to marry me."

"It's just a temporary thing," Jake said. "Believe me. The next time, you'll be fine."

"It's not like I didn't want to," Sam said. "I mean, Emma is hot. She's got this great body and the way she kisses me just gets me going. You know what that's like, right?"

Jake bit his bottom lip and forced a smile, his mind rewinding back to the afternoon he'd spent with Caley. "Yeah, I know what that's like," he muttered.

"She and Caley are going out tomorrow night," Sam said. "Girl's night out. I know I don't have to worry about that. If Caley is there, nothing is going to happen to Emma. But what if Emma starts looking around for a guy who can…do it?"

"Maybe we should go out," Jake suggested. "Take your mind off of your troubles. Just the best man and the groom, some male bonding."

"Yeah," Sam said. "I'm twenty-one now. I can get into any bar."

"And I've got just the place." Jake stood and grabbed his jeans from the floor. "Listen, you can hang out here tonight. There's sheets and blankets for the sofa bed in the closet. I'm just going to run back up to the house and get us something to drink and then we can talk. We'll get this all sorted out."

"Thanks," Sam said. "I don't know what I'd do without you. Maybe, someday, when you get married, I can return the favor."

Jake slipped into his shirt, then pulled on his socks and boots. "I'll be back," he said as he headed for the door. "Just relax."

He jogged down the stairs, then walked across the lawn toward his parents' house. Jake pulled his cell phone from his pocket and dialed Caley's number. She didn't answer, her voice message picking up at four rings.

"Hey, there, it's me. Listen, I'm not going to be able to make it tonight. Sam stopped by the boathouse after you left and he needs some company. Man problems. So, I guess I'll see you tomorrow." He paused, holding back the next words he wanted to say. "Sleep tight," Jake finished.

The sentiment had almost come out without a second thought. Love you. That's what he'd wanted to say, what he'd meant to say. But at the last moment, Jake had censored himself, wondering if it was too much too soon. The words didn't always have to have such a serious meaning, did they? He did love Caley, but those feelings had changed and the words had now taken on a much deeper significance.

Being with Caley again had brought back a piece of his life that had been missing. She made him believe it was possible to find a best friend and a lover in one person. And it wasn't a stretch to add wife to that list.

Jake shook his head. He'd never thought much about marriage. Maybe he always knew in some secret corner of his mind that there was only one woman for him. He stopped, then cursed softly. Was it supposed to be this easy? He'd always assumed that it would take forever to fall in love and even longer to figure out whether that love could survive marriage. But suddenly, it all seemed so simple.

Jake's phone rang and he pulled it out of his pocket and squinted at the caller ID. He smiled when he recognized Caley's number.

"Hey," he said. "Did you get my message?"

"Yes. What's going on? What are man problems?"

"A couple days ago, I told Sam if he wanted to have sex before he and Emma were married, he should just tell Emma and they should do it. I guess it didn't go so well."

"How did it not go well? Did Emma refuse?"

"No. She jumped at the chance. She agreed and then they tried and Sam couldn't perform."

"Oh," Caley said. "That's got to be a little scary. I mean, she was holding out, hoping it would be the most wonderful thing in the world and then…" She drew a deep breath. "Thank God this didn't happen on their wedding night. Can you imagine what a disappointment that would have been?"

"So I guess this plays into our plan," Jake said. "They're obviously both having doubts right about now."

A long silence came from the other end of the line and for a moment, Jake thought the call had been dropped. "So we should continue?" she finally asked.

"I guess so," Jake said. "What do we know about their relationship? Hell, we can't even figure out what's going on between us."

"Sex," Caley said. "Lust. Curiosity."

"And that's all?"

"What else would there be?" she replied.

He cursed the fact that they were discussing this over the phone instead of face-to-face. He couldn't read her expression, couldn't look into her eyes for the truth of her words. "You tell me."

"I don't know. What do you want me to say? I don't know what's going on any more than you do. When the week is over, I guess we'll have to figure it all out."

"Right," Jake said. He glanced over his shoulder. "I should go back to Sam. He's going to want to talk and I told him I was going to grab some beer from the house."

"Emma and I are driving into Chicago tomorrow morning," Caley said. "She wants to check on the cake and some friends of hers are throwing a wedding shower. So I guess I'll see you sometime tomorrow night. Enjoy the strip club."

"Are you jealous, Caley?"

"No! I don't care if you look at naked women. Why would that bother me?"

"Because it would be nice if you were a little jealous. I'd like to think that you care enough about me to be worried."

"Maybe I'll have to give you a lap dance the next time I see you," she said in a teasing voice.

"Thanks for the image," he murmured. "Now I'm never going to get to sleep."

"Good night, Jake."

"Good night, Caley." He waited until she hung up before he switched off his phone. This was a strange, new feeling, Jake mused. They were almost acting like a…a couple. And even more surprising was that Jake didn't mind it at all. He wanted Caley to feel possessive and jealous and worried. Whether she was willing to admit it, she cared about him, maybe loved him a little bit. And maybe he loved her a little bit, too.

5

"I DON'T SEE WHY we had to leave. I was having a good time," Sam complained, his words slurred by all the beer he'd drunk.

Jake glanced over at his little brother. He'd never expected Sam to enjoy himself as much as he had. In truth, Jake had thought they'd spend an hour at the club and then head over to Tyler's to find the girls. Jake had finally convinced Sam to drag himself away from the dazzling charms of Tiffany Diamond and check up on his fiancée.

Though Caley might be worried about his night with naked women, Jake had much more cause to worry about her. He knew how he felt. She was the one who'd just dumped her boyfriend and tumbled into bed with the first man who tried to seduce her. Although Jake would like to believe Caley only had eyes for him, a few fruity drinks and some male attention could do a lot to a girl's memory.

"You know those girls were only being friendly

to you because you were buying them champagne. They get a cut of everything you spend on them."

"But they were nice," Sam said. "Especially that Tiffany. She's going to meet us at Tyler's."

"You invited a stripper to meet us?" Jake shook his head. This was in addition to the Wedding Trasher plan. Stripper and fiancée meet. Jake wasn't sure any relationship could weather that particular event.

"Tiffany Diamond. Do you think that's her real name?"

He was actually beginning to feel a bit guilty about the evening, but this was ridiculous. If his little brother was this naive about strippers, then he had absolutely no business getting married. There were certain things a guy needed to know and Sam's education had obviously fallen woefully short. "Have you ever been to a strip club?" Jake asked.

"Sure," Sam mumbled, resting his head on the cold window. "But never one where the strippers were so nice. Do you think Emma would mind if I invited Tiffany to the wedding?"

"No," Jake said. "I'm sure she wouldn't mind. And Mom would be thrilled to meet her, too. Maybe she could wear that little outfit that she danced in."

"You know, she doesn't want to be a stripper all her life," Sam said. "She actually wants to be a professional cheerleader. Or a dancer in Vegas."

"Please tell me it's the liquor talking," Jake murmured.

"Yeah, it's the liquor talking," Sam said. "But I'm moving my own lips."

The next time Jake glanced over at Sam, he was asleep, his face smashed against the frosty window, his breath creating a tiny clear spot. Jake had to wonder about the sense of this plan that he and Caley had set in motion. When booze was mixed into the equation, there was every chance that things could go bad very quickly. Add a stripper to the mix and disaster was guaranteed. Were he and Caley really ready to deal with the fallout from this evening? Jake wondered. And would this be a true test of the commitment between Sam and Emma or just a blatant manipulation?

When he reached Tyler's Roadhouse, Jake pulled into a far corner of the parking lot. But instead of waking Sam up, he decided to go inside and find Caley and call this whole thing off. They'd gone far enough and it was time to put this wedding back in Sam and Emma's hands. He didn't want to spend the rest of their week together thinking about Sam and Emma. He wanted to focus on Caley.

Jake quietly slipped out of the truck and locked the door behind him. Though it was cold out, Sam could survive for the five minutes it would take to grab Caley and Emma and convince them to go home.

Jake paid the cover charge at the door, then pushed through the crowd, squinting in the dark to locate the Lambert sisters. He immediately saw Emma on the dance floor, dressed in a shockingly sexy outfit of skintight jeans, a sheer blouse and some kind of underwear beneath it.

She was dancing with a scruffy-looking young man in a backward baseball cap, the two of them laughing and waving their arms along with a Bruce Springsteen song. Jake's gaze continued to skim the crowd and he saw Caley standing near the edge of the dance floor. He cursed softly when he saw Jeff Winslow standing next to her.

Jake felt his fingers clench into a fist. Why did that guy get on his nerves so much? It was obvious from the way they were standing that there was nothing going on between them. But still, he'd never liked competing for Caley's attention, even when they were kids. And he liked it a lot less now that they were adults.

He wove through the patrons until he stepped up beside her. "Caley," he shouted. She jumped at first at the sound of his voice, but when she turned and saw him, Caley gave him a smile of relief. "Hey, Winslow," he said, giving the cop a nod.

Jeff smiled. "You two better take that girl home,"

he said, pointing at Emma with the neck of his beer bottle. "I think she's had enough."

"Where is Sam?" Caley shouted.

"In the car. Drunk and asleep." He took her hand and pulled her along toward the door. When they got there, he glanced back at Jeff Winslow. The guy didn't look happy, but he hadn't tried to stop Caley from leaving. Then he looked at Emma. "She looks like she's having a little too much fun."

Caley nodded. "That's because she's had a little too much tequila. It won't seem like fun in the morning. She's dancing with some guy named Robert. He seems harmless enough."

They stepped outside into the chilly night air and walked around the corner of the building. The moment they reached a private spot, Jake grabbed Caley, pressed her back against the wall and kissed her. It wasn't an expression of lust or even affection. He needed reassurance that nothing had changed in the hours that they'd been apart. When she responded, Jake felt an overwhelming sense of relief.

"That's better," he murmured. His hand slipped beneath her jacket and slowly searched for bare skin. When he found it, he splayed his hand across the small of her back. "You're so warm."

Caley shivered, her teeth chattering. "Not for long. My car is parked over there. Let's get out of the cold." She handed Jake the keys and they hurried over to the spot where she'd left the rental. Jake let her in the passenger side and then hopped behind the wheel. He started the engine and turned on the heater. "It'll take a while to warm up."

"I'm starting to think this whole thing was a really bad idea," Caley said, rubbing her hands together.

Jake took her fingers between his and blew on them. "Me, too."

"What ever made us think this was the right thing to do?"

"Maybe we're transferring our own fears about commitment to Sam and Emma. I mean, they seem to know what they're doing and we haven't had much success in that department."

"Well, a little success," Caley murmured, staring at her fingers as he kissed each one. "Just since we came home."

Jake smiled and pressed her hands to his chest. "Yeah. A little. More than a little, I'd say." He reached out and slipped his hand around her waist, pulled her closer. He'd spent the evening looking at naked women and he hadn't been the slightest bit affected. But the moment he touched Caley, his desire warmed and his pulse raced.

"Do you think if we crawled in the back seat and took all our clothes off anyone would notice?" Jake murmured. "People make love in roadhouse parking lots all the time."

Caley laughed. "Don't you think it would be easier if we just went back to the inn?"

"Only if you do that lap dance you promised me," he said.

"All right," Caley replied. "I think I can do that."

"We'll go inside, get Emma, then dump them both in Emma's room at the inn and let them figure this out for themselves."

"Good plan."

They both jumped out of the car and hurried back to the front door, but a small crowd had gathered outside. "What's going on?" Jake asked.

"There's a fight," one of the girls said. "Some guy and his fiancée and a stripper."

Jake groaned. "Oh, hell." He turned to Caley. "You stay here. I'll be right back." An instant later, the sounds of a siren could be heard in the distance.

"Get Emma," Caley cried. "Before she gets hurt."

Jake pressed through the crush of people leaving the bar and when he finally got inside, the place was lit up and emptied of half the patrons. The band was lounging around the stage and a small group was gathered in the middle of the dance floor. Emma and Sam were sitting on the floor, Tiffany was holding her nose and arguing with Jeff Winslow and a guy that Jake recognized as Emma's dance partner was laid out flat in front of them all, his hands clutching his crotch.

Jake strode up to group. "What's going on here?"

"Just step back," Winslow warned. "Everything is under control."

"This is my brother and my future sister-in-law. I want to take them home."

Winslow glanced over his shoulder at Jake and shook his head. "I'm going to have to take your brother and his fiancée in. They started this brawl. Assault, public intoxication—"

"They're in a bar," Jake said. "Everyone is intoxicated."

"You can meet them down at the station. We'll get things sorted out there."

"Come on," Jake said. "Don't be a hard-ass, Winslow. No one was seriously hurt here."

"She hit me in the nose!" Tiffany cried.

"She ran into my elbow," Emma countered. "I was trying to help Robert up after Sam kicked him in the crotch. And she got in the way."

"I didn't kick him," Sam said.

"Yeah, you did, man," Robert groaned from the floor.

Sam shrugged. "It was a knee to the crotch, not a kick."

"Isn't there just a fine I can pay right away and we can take care of this mess without wasting any more time?" Jake asked.

"What's going on here?" They all turned to look

at Caley as she joined the group, a worried expression furrowing her brow.

"I'm breaking up with Sam," Emma announced. "We're not getting married."

"You can't break up with me," Sam countered, "because I already broke up with you."

Emma sent him a withering glare. "You have no reason to break up with me. I was just dancing with Robert. I wasn't dancing *on* him like that stripper was doing to you."

"I'm not a stripper," Tiffany said. "I prefer exotic dancer."

"You invited her to our wedding!" Emma cried. "Sometimes, I wonder if you even have a brain in your head."

"And sometimes I wonder if you have a heart," Sam shot back.

"Enough!" Winslow shouted. "There will be no more talking. Or I'll throw all of you behind bars."

"Can I go now?" Robert asked. "I've got to start packing up the van. I'm with the band." He slowly got to his feet, wincing slightly as he straightened. "I'm not going to press charges."

"Neither am I," Tiffany said. She wandered over to Robert and smiled coyly. "So you're with the band? I love musicians."

The pair wandered off toward the stage and Officer

Winslow started after them. Then he turned and pointed to Emma and Sam. "Don't move," he ordered.

Jake glanced over at Caley and shrugged. "Maybe you can talk to him. He seems to like you more than he likes me." He watched as Caley tried to plead their case. Though he hated sending her back to Winslow, he was certain there'd be no chance she'd be leaving with him.

A few seconds later, Caley returned, a satisfied smile on her face. "We can take them home," she murmured. "He's letting them off, but only if they agree to stay out of trouble for the rest of their time here."

"What did you have to promise him in return?" Jake asked.

"Nothing. He's doing it as a favor to me."

Jake cursed softly and looked down at Sam and Emma. "It would probably do them some good to spend a night in jail."

Caley shook her head and held out her hand to her sister. "Come on. Let's get out of here. I'll take Emma back to the inn and you bring Sam."

Sam also stumbled to his feet and brushed his jeans off. "This is all your fault," he muttered to Jake. "We should have just stayed at the strip club. I was having fun there."

They walked out to the parking lot together, Sam and Emma silent and sullen with Jake and Caley standing between them. As Caley started toward her car, Jake grabbed her hand. "I'll see you later?" he asked.

Caley nodded then walked away, slipping her arm around Emma's shoulders as they walked off. Sam stared after them, an enigmatic expression on his face.

"You're not really going to call off the wedding, are you?" Jake asked.

"I think we are," he murmured, before he turned in the opposite direction.

They didn't speak during the ride home, Sam lost in his thoughts and Jake unwilling to meddle even further. Though he and Caley had achieved their goal, now that the wedding was off, Jake wondered whether they'd gone too far.

While his feelings for Caley ran deep, he knew that they were also very fragile; would they suffer at the first test or would they endure? He knew how he felt, but he still couldn't be sure of Caley's feelings. Now that he'd fallen, Jake was wondering if the risk was worth the reward. Losing Caley would be much more difficult the second time around.

WHEN CALEY FINALLY RETURNED to her room at the inn, Jake was asleep in her bed, his naked body twisted in the sheets, his hair falling in waves across his forehead. Caley stripped off her clothes and tossed them against the wall, crinkling her nose at the scent of stale beer and cigarette smoke.

She glanced over at the clock on the nightstand and sighed softly. It was nearly 3:00 a.m. She'd spent the past three hours with Emma, trying to convince her to reconsider canceling the wedding and listing all of Sam's good qualities over and over again.

She couldn't believe Emma was so quick to dismiss her engagement. Caley realized that emotions ran much higher with all the alcohol that had been consumed, but Emma seemed perfectly lucid and determined to leave Sam and her wedding plans behind. She'd even called the airline to buy a ticket back to Boston on the first flight out in the morning.

Did anyone ever find a lasting love? Or was it all just an illusion, as shiny and clear as glass until something came along to shatter it? Did people stay in relationships only because they were too stubborn to admit defeat?

Caley knew her parents loved each other. They'd been together almost thirty years. And Jake's parents often acted like newlyweds. So why was it so hard for her to believe in love?

She walked to the bathroom and closed the door behind her, then turned on the shower, ignoring the urge to crawl into bed with Jake. It would be so easy to find comfort in his arms. She felt safe with him. But were her feelings real or were they just part of a fantasy that she was only now having the chance to live out?

There was no doubt in her mind that everything

between them had changed. He'd become a part of her life and not a part she could easily excise. In truth, she couldn't imagine living without him. Yet, she couldn't quite figure out how she could live with him.

How would it work? Would they call it an affair? A relationship? An arrangement? Friends with benefits, she mused. That's what they had now, wasn't it? But for them to continue, they'd have to give it a name.

A soft knock sounded on the bathroom door before it slowly opened. Jake stepped inside, his naked body beautiful in even the harsh fluorescent light. He slipped his arms around her waist and kissed her forehead.

"Is everything all right?"

"I just needed to take a shower. I smell like smoke."

"How's Emma?"

"Still drunk, still furious with Sam and ready to go back to Boston in the morning."

Jake took her hand and pulled her along to the shower stall, then opened the glass door. He stepped inside, the water hitting his naked body and sluicing over his skin. Caley followed him, stepping right into his embrace.

His fingers furrowed through her hair and he kissed her, his tongue slipping between her lips to taste her mouth. The moment their bodies touched, every doubt and insecurity seemed to vanish. Why was it so easy to believe in love when they were making love and so hard to understand it when they were apart?

Jake drew back and stared down into her eyes, then reached out to touch her breast. He cupped her warm flesh gently, running his thumb over her nipple until it became a stiff peak. Then he smoothed his hand along her hip, his fingers soft and teasing.

Caley reached out and brushed her fingers against his hard shaft. It had taken only a moment for him to become aroused and she found her power over him satisfying. Jake moaned softly as she wrapped her fingers around his heat.

Already, his body was so familiar to her. She knew how he'd react to her touch, the way his breath would catch in his throat, the sound of his voice whispering her name, the feel of his body tensing just before he reached his release.

Jake grabbed her waist and slowly backed her up against the tile wall of the shower. He kissed the curve of her neck and then moved lower, teasing at her nipple with his tongue. "Tell me what you want," he murmured as he gently caressed her nipple.

"You," she said. "Inside me."

He dropped his hand to the soft curve of her backside and gently squeezed. "Tell me how."

"First, you have to kiss me in just the right way."

Jake gave it his best effort, kissing her gently at

first and then with growing urgency, dragging his tongue along the crease of her mouth until she surrendered completely. Her knees went soft and she felt herself melt in his arms, the warm water rushing over them both.

"That's a start," she murmured.

Jake slowly trailed kisses over her shoulder and down her arm. When he knelt in front of her, Caley raked her fingers through his wet hair, pulling him away when his tongue tickled.

He was so beautiful, so incredibly sexy. She couldn't imagine ever feeling this attracted to another man. There seemed to be electricity that crackled between them every time they were together. Just one touch of his fingers to her bare skin was all it took for the attraction to overwhelm them both.

Jake's lips trailed lower, until he found the dampness between her legs. She was already aroused and the moment he touched her there, her body jerked in response. "I love that I can touch you like this," he murmured. "That there's nothing left to stop us." He gently parted her legs, tasting her until she writhed against him.

"Oh," she breathed. "Oh, right there."

As he brought her closer and closer to her release, Caley murmured his name urgently, her fingers twisted tightly in his hair. Jake followed her cues, dragging her back from the edge when she got too close. It wasn't enough. She didn't want to experience this pleasure by herself.

She drew him back to his feet, tugging gently on his hair until he stood in front of her. Jake knew what she wanted without her even needing to tell him. He stepped back and gave her a crooked smile. "I have to go get a condom."

Caley grabbed his hand and shook her head. "It's all right," she said. "You don't have to worry."

"Are you sure?"

Caley nodded. She'd been on the pill for years and it had always seemed like such a practical thing. But now, it was liberating. She trusted Jake and he trusted her. She wanted to experience him without any barriers between them. And if they had this one night together, this chance to possess each other completely, then it would be enough. Caley didn't care what came later as long as this came now.

She turned off the shower, then pulled him along to the bed, their bodies dripping water on the carpet. She lay back on the mattress and Jake braced himself above her. Gently, she guided him to her entrance and he closed his eyes the moment they touched.

Slowly, exquisitely, he pushed inside of her, filling her inch by inch until he was buried deep. Caley felt the muscles in his body tense, but he didn't give in. Instead, he began to move.

She closed her eyes and focused on the sensations that washed over her body. She was already so close, but this seemed to take her to a higher level, the need growing more intense with each stroke. This was paradise, she thought. There was nothing more perfect. Every year that had passed since that night of her eighteenth birthday had led them to this moment.

"I want you," he murmured. "Come for me."

He increased his pace and Caley felt herself dancing on the edge. And when her release came, it came so fast that it caught her by surprise. She cried out and the pleasure shook her body, stealing her ability to think.

It was enough to send him over the edge and Jake surrendered a moment later. It was simple, uncomplicated and pure, the two of them searching for release and finding it with each other.

He was like an addiction, a craving that she could only satisfy for a short time. Though she felt sated now, Caley knew she'd want more, each time searching for that certainty, that knowledge that this was something that might last. He rolled over, gathering her in his arms and nuzzling into the curve of her neck. "Can we stay here forever?" he murmured.

"I think the maid will probably discover us when she comes to make the bed and do the vacuuming," Caley joked.

Jake pushed up on his elbow. "You're supposed

to say yes," he teased. "Or I'll feel as if you weren't well satisfied."

"I was," she said.

They lay together, wrapped in each other's arms, for a long time. Caley listened to his breathing. He wasn't asleep and she wondered what he was thinking. But she was afraid to ask. They'd so carefully avoided the subject of the future, but it was coming at them quickly.

"What are we going to do about Emma and Sam?" she asked. "We're going to have to figure out a way to get them back together."

"I know."

Caley nodded. "I think they might actually love each other. And if it weren't for our meddling, this wouldn't have happened. So we have to fix it." She drew a ragged breath. "We have to."

"All right," Jake said, his hand slowly caressing her breast. "How are we going to do that?"

"I don't know. We have to make them want each other, the way we want each other."

"I don't think there's another man on the planet who wants a woman the way I want you," Jake murmured.

"Don't you wonder?" Caley said. "Is this un-usual? Are we an…aberration?"

Jake answered before he even considered her question. "This is the way it was meant to be with us," he said.

"What are we going to do when this is over?"

The question seemed to take him by surprise and this time, he didn't have a quick and easy answer. "I don't know, Caley," he said. "I don't want to think about that."

"Promise me this," she said. "Promise me that before either one of us begins a life with someone else, that we'll meet back here and be together, just to be sure."

"I promise," he said. "We can come every summer and we can stay at Havenwoods. No one will know we're here. And it'll be just us. For as long as we're both…free."

Caley snuggled up against his body, pressing her face into his warm skin. It was enough for now, she thought to herself. She would have time to figure out how she felt, time to see if this need for Jake would fade with time and distance between them. And if it didn't, then Jake would be there for her. He'd promised.

JAKE AWOKE WITH A START. Caley shook him again and he turned to look at her. "What?" he murmured, rubbing his eyes.

"Wake up. It's nine in the morning. We overslept."

Jake rolled over on his stomach and snuggled into the pillows on Caley's bed. "I'm going to sleep in. I had a late night last night."

"And what are you going to tell your mother when she finds you missing?"

"I'm going to tell her that I drove into Chicago early to check up on things at the office and then stopped for breakfast on the way home. So we actually have the entire morning to spend in bed. It's a two-hour drive each way plus an hour at the office and another hour at breakfast."

Caley smiled. "And what if they see your truck in the parking lot?"

"I parked in back," Jake said.

"All right. I give up," Caley said. "We can spend the morning in bed."

Jake grinned and dropped a kiss on each naked breast. "Good. I knew you wouldn't need a lot of convincing."

She curled back up beside him, wrapping her arms around her waist. Suddenly, she drew in a sharp breath. "We can't stay in bed. We have to fix Emma and Sam." Throwing aside the covers, she stumbled to her feet, then searched the room for her clothes.

Caley's hair was wild around her face. She'd gone to bed with it wet and it had dried into a mass of waves and curls. "Emma said she was going to leave this morning. She may already be gone. And Sam has probably spilled the beans to the family. We have to fix that first, then we'll deal with us later."

Jake closed his eyes, his mind skipping back to the

events of the previous evening. He wondered how long it would take for news of the canceled wedding to work its way through the Burtbert grapevine. Sam was probably sleeping off his hangover, but once he got up, he'd inform everyone of the details—including the roles Jake and Caley had played in the breakup.

Jake tossed back the covers. "What do you suggest we do?"

"I was hoping you'd have an idea. We don't have a lot of time left," Caley said.

Jake smoothed his hand over her thigh, then moved higher, wondering if he might tempt her just a little bit. Caley closed her eyes and moaned softly. "Don't," she whispered.

"I have to," Jake replied.

"You have to go talk to Sam," she said.

He slid his fingers into her dampness. "I will, as soon as I take care of this."

"We'll have time for this later," she whispered. "I promise."

Jake was well aware of how much time they had left. A week had seemed like forever when he'd first found her in bed with him. But the days seemed to dissolve in front of him until he was faced with the fact that there would be an end to this fantasy.

"Not later," he said. "Now." He grabbed her waist and pulled her on top of him, then caught her wrists behind her back. "Tell me you want me." Jake pulled her down into a long, deep kiss. "Say it and I'll let you go."

"I do want you," Caley murmured. She shifted above him, his hard shaft pressed between her legs. "I do."

Jake released her wrists, but Caley didn't move away. Instead, she raked her hands through his hair and returned his kiss, her tongue teasing at his. It was as if she'd sensed his desperation, heard the clock ticking on their time together. It was the end of the summer again, Jake thought to himself. It had happened every year, the waning season stealing her away from him once again. But this time would be different. This time, he could ask her to stay.

Jake cupped her face in his hands and looked into her sleepy gaze. "What are we going to do about this?" he murmured. "Tell me."

Caley reached for him and a moment later he was inside her. "We can do anything we want," she said as she lowered herself on top of him. "We're not kids anymore."

They made love slowly, building the passion between them with soft kisses and gentle caresses. As he touched her, Jake memorized the feel of her body, the sound of her voice. After she was gone, he wanted to recall every detail. And when they finally surrendered to each other, it was as it had been from the start—perfect.

As she snuggled against his chest, Jake buried his face in Caley's hair, breathing in the scent of her shampoo. There were so many things he had to say to her, but he just couldn't seem to put them into coherent sentences. He wanted to tell her how much she meant to him. He wanted to promise her that they'd be together forever, no matter what happened. But he was afraid that saying too much too soon might scare her away rather than bring her closer.

"If only Emma and Sam were doing what we are right now," Caley murmured. "We wouldn't need to fix anything."

"Maybe there's a way to get them there," Jake said, toying with a strand of her hair. "If you wanted to plan the perfect seduction, what would you need?"

"You'd have to have a location where you'd be completely alone with nothing to disturb you," Caley began.

"We have that. Havenwoods. What else?"

"Champagne, good things to eat, a fireplace." Caley giggled. "Whipped cream, honey, chocolate syrup."

"You've got to have sexy underwear," Jake said. "I love those, what do you call them, they hold up stockings?"

"Garter belts," Caley said. "All men love those."

"Is there anyplace in town where you can get those? And black fishnet stockings. And one of those push-up bras. And a thong."

"I can see your evening at the strip club has

made you an expert. Most women think those things are trashy. They want something pretty, feminine…but sexy."

Jake crawled out of bed, then grabbed his boxers and pulled them on. If he didn't get dressed, he'd never get out of Caley's bed. "I'll buy the champagne and the groceries. You find the lingerie. Then you get Emma and I'll grab Sam and I'll meet you at noon at Havenwoods. We'll lock them in and we won't let them out until they work out all their issues."

"And what will we do?"

"We'll sit back and wait," Jake said, "and hope that at least some of our sexual DNA is pumping through their veins."

A knock sounded on her room door and Caley bolted upright, her eyes wide. "Yes?"

"Caley? It's Emma. I'm packed and I'm ready to leave. I was hoping you might take me to the airport."

"What time is your flight?"

"It's later this afternoon. But I want to go. I don't want to see Sam."

"Just give me a minute," Caley said. "I'll meet you downstairs. We'll have some breakfast."

"All right," Emma said.

Caley threw on her clothes, then raked her fingers through her tangled hair. "All right. I think I can stall her. But you're going to have to do the shopping. Don't get fishnets or a thong. Just get a pretty camisole and some sexy panties. There's a bath store just a few doors down from that restaurant with the cinnamon buns. They'll be open in an hour. I'll call and tell them what you need. Then, I'll bring Emma out to Havenwoods at noon."

Jake grabbed her around the waist and gave her a long, lingering kiss. "Noon," he said. "Once we get them settled, then you and I are going to spend the rest of the afternoon together."

Caley drew a deep breath and moved toward the door. But Jake caught her fingers in his and she turned to look at him. "What?"

"I'm glad we didn't do it that night on the beach," he said.

"You are?"

"It wouldn't have been like this," he said.

"Nothing has ever been quite like this," she admitted.

Jake drew his thumb across her lower lip, then kissed her again. "Sometimes I wonder, though. I wonder if we would have done it, maybe we would have been the two getting married instead of Sam and Emma. Maybe it would have been the start of something for us." He chuckled softly. "Maybe we were supposed to be together and we just got it all wrong."

"Or maybe we'd be the ones having doubts," Caley said.

Jake smiled, then waited as she walked out. It was no longer possible to separate his life from Caley's. Every thought of the future, whether it was a day away or years away, always came back to her.

6

"I THINK THEY'LL BE ALL RIGHT," Emma said. "Mama seemed upset, but I don't think she'd want me to get married just so she won't have to waste all that lobster we ordered."

Caley glanced both ways, then pulled the car out onto the road into North Lake. She'd agreed to drive Emma to the airport to catch her flight back to Boston under the condition that Emma go to the lake house first and explain what had happened to the family. Now that she'd completed that task, there would be one more little detour.

"Don't you think you're being a bit hasty about this, Emma? You were drunk last night and you and Sam haven't even tried to work this out."

"Sam is an idiot," Emma said. "And I need to get back to Boston. I don't know what ever made me think we were meant for each other. I'm young. I should be out there exploring my options, not tying myself down with a guy who socializes with strippers."

"Sam had a little too much to drink. And I think it would be silly to throw your relationship away over one little indiscretion." Caley paused. "He didn't cheat, he was just being friendly. Instead of running away from your problems, you and Sam need to put some serious thought into what you both expect from marriage. But that takes discussion, not a drunken brawl at a roadhouse and you running off to Boston."

"I don't want to talk to him," Emma said stubbornly.

"Do you still love him?"

Emma turned her head away and stared out the window. "I don't know."

They drove through town in silence and headed out on the East Shore Road, Caley watching for the sign for Havenwoods. It was only a few minutes before Emma realized that they weren't traveling toward the interstate. "Where are we going?"

"I want to show you something," Caley said. "Jake showed it to me a few days ago." She turned into the drive and carefully navigated the curves down to the main house.

"What is this?"

"You'll see," Caley said.

She stopped the car in front of the house. Jake emerged from the house, stepping out onto the wide porch. A few moments later, Sam appeared in the doorway. Emma glanced over at Caley then looked out the window at her former fiancé. "What's going on?"

"You and Sam need to talk. Jake and I thought it would be best if you had a place where you could be completely alone and undisturbed."

"I have a plane to catch," Emma insisted.

"That can wait."

"What is this place? Some kind of haunted house?"

"It's not as bad as it looks. It's quiet and secluded. And kind of romantic." Caley got out of the car, giving Emma no choice but to follow. When she joined Jake on the porch, he handed her the bag from the lingerie shop.

"I couldn't resist the garter belt," he murmured.

Emma joined them on the porch and Caley passed the bag to her. "You might need this," she said.

Emma peered inside, then withdrew a sexy black camisole and panties, followed by the garter belt and black stockings. "I thought you said we were supposed to talk."

"This is meant to help the conversation along."

"Hello, Emma," Sam said, stepping out of the doorway onto the porch. His gaze searched her face, but she refused to look at him.

"Hello, idiot," she muttered.

"Rule number one," Jake said. "No name-calling." He started down the length of the porch, then motioned Sam and Emma to follow. When they reached the lake side of the house, they walked down the snow-packed path to the summer kitchen. "All right. You'll stay here until you've worked things out. When you've both come to a rational decision about your future together, you can leave a lantern burning in the window and we'll come and get you. There's food and firewood inside. There's a bathroom through the small door near the fireplace. I want you both to go inside, take off your jackets, your shoes and the rest of your clothes and put them on the porch. I'll give them back to you when it's time to leave."

"What?" Sam said.

"I'm not giving you my clothes," Emma said.

"Do we really need their clothes?" Caley asked.

"They can't run away if we have their clothes," Jake explained. "Unless they want to trudge through the snow in their bare feet, they won't be going anywhere."

"I'm not going to marry him," Emma said. "You could lock me up and throw away the key and I still wouldn't change my mind."

"I wouldn't marry her if she were the last person on earth," Sam countered.

"Fine," Jake said. "If that's what you decide. But you're going to come out of this with an understanding and a respect for each other. Our families have been friends for years and you're not going to mess this up because you both want to carry a grudge. You're the pair who started this and if you're going to end it, then do it right. Either you leave here as two friends or as two people about to be married, I don't care which."

"Where are we supposed to sleep?" Sam asked.

"There's a cot inside and warm blankets."

"I'll just call someone to come and get us."

"There's no phone inside," Jake said. "And I have your cell phone. You lent it to me earlier this morning. And Caley borrowed Emma's phone. You'll talk to each other and that's it. Now, Caley and I will be back to check up on you tomorrow morning."

"You can't do this," Sam said. "You're supposed to be on my side."

Jake shrugged. "Yeah, I can do this."

"Caley, you can't leave me here," Emma said.

"Maybe we should let them keep their clothes," Caley suggested. "The jackets and pants and shoes will be enough to keep them from running away."

"I wouldn't bet on it," Sam muttered. "You know, when the owner finds out that you kept us here, there'll be trouble. I could charge you with—with kidnapping. Or unlawful imprisonment. Or—or—"

"I know the owner and he won't mind," Jake said. "Now get inside and start undressing."

Grudgingly, Emma and Sam disappeared inside the summer kitchen and a few minutes later, they tossed their jackets, pants and shoes out onto the porch. Caley gave Jake an optimistic smile. "That didn't go so badly."

"Maybe we should wait around for a little while just to make sure they don't kill each other."

"Good idea."

Jake grabbed her hand and they walked back to the main house. He opened the front door and she walked inside. Caley looked at the house differently now that she knew it was Jake's home. She could imagine herself there on a warm summer day, all the windows thrown open to catch the breeze. The birds would sing from the trees and at night the leaves would rustle. She closed her eyes and inhaled the scent, determined to remember it.

"I love this place. I can just imagine what it was like years ago, without television and speedboats and electricity. It must have been so relaxing to live that way. To just slow down and let life happen."

"I've thought about restoring the place to its original state," Jake said, stepping behind her and slipping his arms around her waist.

His touch sent her pulse racing and she leaned back against him and smiled. "Really? You could live like that?"

"I wouldn't take out the electricity and the plumbing. I think the lack of conveniences might wear a little thin, especially in the middle of winter. I'd be chopping firewood twenty-four hours a day just to stay warm. But it would be all right to just turn it all off."

"Maybe for a day. But I really like a hot shower in the morning."

He rested his chin on her shoulder. "What happened to your sense of adventure? You've gotten to be very high maintenance, haven't you?"

Caley turned in his arms. "I'm still adventurous. And there are things you can do in a shower that you can't do washing up in the sink."

He growled softly, remembering their late-night lovemaking. "Yeah, I can see that. But skinny-dipping in the lake could be lots of fun, too."

"So what are we going to do here? We gave Sam and Emma the only bed."

Jake kissed her neck. "I was going to go up to the attic and look for the doors to the sun porch," he said. "Or we can find something more interesting to do. The grease trap in the sink needs to be cleaned. And I think there's a dead mouse in the linen closet."

"Let's go up in the attic," Caley said.

"There may be spiders. Or bats."

"It'll be an adventure," she teased.

Jake fetched a flashlight from the kitchen and they walked to the rear bedroom. He opened a door to reveal a stairway. They'd explored every inch of this house when they were kids, but Caley didn't remember ever venturing into the attic. "Have you been up here?"

"A couple of times," he said. "Watch out. The stairs are steep. You go first."

Caley stared up into the dark attic and shook her head. "You go first."

"You're the adventurous one."

"It's your house."

"I'll give you a hundred dollars if you go first."

Caley rolled her eyes. "What a baby you are." She squinted up into the darkness. "What are you looking for?"

"Doors. There should be two doors that used to hang in the entrances to the solarium. The doors that are there are too new. They have beveled glass windows, which isn't something that Durant would have chosen. I'm hoping the originals are up there."

The attic wasn't nearly as bad as Caley thought it would be. Though everything was covered with a thick coating of dust, it was tidy and snug. "I wonder what's in these trunks."

Jake shrugged. "Probably something creepy."

"Like what? A dead body?" Caley knelt down on the floor. "Hold the flashlight on this latch," she said.

"The doors won't be in there. They're huge."

"I know. But aren't you curious as to what's in here? It might be something interesting." Caley tugged at the latch and it flipped open. "If there's a skeleton in here, I'm going to scream."

"So am I," Jake said.

But when Caley opened the trunk, she found it filled with bundles of letters and greeting cards, old

gramophone records and books. She pulled out one
of the books and flipped through it. "It's a journal,"
she said. She grabbed a bigger book and found pho-
tographs inside. Caley handed it to Jake, then
glanced around the attic. "Is there a gramophone up
here?"

Jake scanned the room with the flashlight, letting
it come to rest on a covered silhouette on a table. "I
think that's it. Can we look for my doors?"

"This is more interesting than your doors," she
said. Caley pointed to the far wall. "Is that them?"

Jake grinned. "I think so. Come on, let's see if we
can get them downstairs."

"Forget the doors right now." She walked around
the chest. "If you pick up that end, I bet we could get
it downstairs."

They wrestled the trunk to the stairway and ma-
neuvered it around the old wooden banister. But as
they began to take it down the steep stairs, Caley lost
her grip. The leather handle had deteriorated with
age and it broke; the trunk slammed down on her
toes.

"Ow! Oh, that hurts. Pull it down."

Jake let the trunk slide to the bottom of the stairs,
then climbed up to where she stood. "What's wrong?"

"It smashed my toe. Ow." Her eyes watered and
she wriggled on her good foot, afraid to put weight
on the other.

Jake stared at the toe of her boot with the flashlight, then cursed softly. "Come on. I think I have some first-aid stuff in the kitchen."

He helped her down the stairs, Caley limping and wincing against the pain. Then Jake scooped her up in his arms and carried her the rest of the way, setting her down on the counter in the kitchen. "I'd forgotten what a klutz you could be."

"I'm not," she said. "I'm very graceful."

"I remember the time you were walking down the dock in that little flowered dress and those high-heeled shoes." He pulled off her boot and tossed it aside. "You got your heel caught in between the boards and went over the edge into the water. I had to jump in and fish you out."

"I was mortified," Caley said. "I wanted you to look at me and think I was hot. Instead, I looked like a drowned rat."

"Maybe so, but when that dress got wet, you could see right through it. And you weren't wearing a bra. I did think you looked really hot."

She pulled her foot out of his hand and tugged off her sock. Her toenail had already begun to turn black. "Kiss it," she said, wiggling her toes in front of him.

Jake smiled, taking her foot in his hand and slowly massaging it. "Will that make it feel better?"

"Maybe. I've always wanted you to kiss my feet," she said, daring him to do as she asked.

Jake knelt down in front of her and pressed his lips to her ankle. It didn't take long for Caley to realize that he was turning her little game into a full-out seduction. He kissed each toe, then ran his tongue along her instep.

When he began to suck on her toes, Caley closed her eyes and leaned back. No man had ever done this for her. She hadn't realized that the foot was an erogenous zone. "Oh," she said.

"Do you like that?" he asked.

"Yes," she murmured.

"Does it feel better?"

Caley nodded. "Much."

Jake stood and ran his thumb along her lower lip. He bent close and kissed her. "Is there anything else that hurts?"

"Are you trying to seduce me?" she asked.

"Maybe. Do you want to be seduced?"

"Yes," Caley said with a smile. "See, isn't that easy? Just think of what might have happened if you'd said yes the first time I asked."

"I was tempted," he said, pulling her hand up to kiss her palm. "So tempted. You looked so beautiful that night. You were wearing that little lace blouse with blue flowers on the collar."

"You remember that?"

"I remember everything about that night. For the next five years, I'd sit on that spot on the beach and wonder if I'd ever get a chance again."

"I guess you did," Caley said.

"I just assumed you'd always be around. When you didn't come back that next summer, I thought I'd messed up bad. Now that I have you again, it's going to be hard to let you go."

It was as close to a profession of love as Jake had ever come and the sentiment made her heart ache. When she was young, she used to read all sorts of meanings into the words he spoke to her. But his meaning was clear now. The only problem was, Caley wasn't sure what she could do about it.

"I've got a sleeping bag in the back of my truck. We could put it in front of the fireplace. It's almost as good as a bed."

"I'll meet you there," Caley said. As he walked out of the room, she drew a deep breath. "I'm not going to be able to let you go, either," she murmured.

JAKE STOOD IN THE DOORWAY of the great room, his hands braced on the doorjamb. Caley sat in front of a crackling fire, her naked body wrapped in the sleeping bag. They'd made love twice in front of the fire, first with a frantic passion and then later slowly and playfully, the two of them teasing each other to completion.

The day was entirely theirs now that the wedding had been put on hold. Jake had felt so bad about her toe that he'd gone upstairs to retrieve the photo album and a few packets of letters from the trunk.

Though they'd enjoyed the sexual chemistry between them, the connection that afternoon had been more emotional than physical. Every time he looked at her, Jake realized how special she was. She was smart and funny. And she challenged him, forcing him to see her in a different light. She'd stolen a piece of his heart a long time ago and now Jake was certain that he never wanted it back. As long as Caley cared for him, he'd be a happy man.

"Are you warm enough?" he asked.

She turned and smiled, the light from the fire illuminating her pretty features. "I am. Come and look at this. I found a photo of the summer kitchen."

Jake crossed the room and squatted down next to her, taking the photo from her fingers. "Look at that stove. No wonder they had to put the kitchen in a separate building. One spark from that and this whole place would have been kindling." He stared at the ceiling. "I should probably put some kind of sprinkler system in here. I wouldn't want this place to burn down before I had a chance to pay for it."

"You should really send this stuff back to the family," she said.

"I don't think the owner realized there was anything left in the attic. I think I'll make an inventory and then see what she wants me to send back to her."

"What is her first name?" Caley asked. "Is it Arlene?"

"Yeah," Jake said.

"I've been reading these letters. They're from a boy she met at a summer dance. They had a romance. He was from town. And she lived in Chicago. It looks like they wrote to each other for years." Caley frowned. "There are some here from when he was in the war. And then they just stop. Are there more letters in the trunk?"

"I can go look," Jake said.

"You don't think he died, do you?"

"No," Jake said. "They're probably still in the trunk. I'll go get them."

Jake wandered back to the bedroom, grabbing the flashlight along the way. It felt good to have Caley in his house. It felt right. He could imagine them here together, spending their summers on the lake. Everything would be so much more interesting if she were a part of his life. They'd begin and end each day together and in between, they would swim and cook and make love by the light of the moon.

Jake rummaged through the papers and then found one more packet of letters, this one much smaller and tied with a black ribbon. He brought them back to Caley and sat down beside her.

"See, it's all right."

She stared at the packet as she slowly untied the ribbon. As she read the first letter, Caley slowly shook her head. "No," she murmured. She glanced over at Jake and he saw tears in her eyes. "This one is from his mother. He died in France in 1944." She flipped through the rest of the letters. "These are all from his mother."

Jake reached out and wrapped his arm around her shoulders. "It's all right. Why are you crying?"

"I don't know. It's so sad. They were in love and then they lost their chance to be together."

He kissed the top of her head, unable to soothe her distress. "I guess you have to just appreciate the time you have," he murmured.

Caley nodded, wiping her eyes on the corner of the sleeping bag. "I do appreciate it." She looked at him. "I do."

Smiling, Jake dropped a soft kiss on her lips. "Why don't we get dressed and I'll take you back to the inn. You can have a nice hot bath. We'll pick up a pizza on the way back and we'll spend the night watching movies."

Caley put the letter back in the envelope and retied the ribbon. He pulled her to her feet and helped her get dressed, wiping away the tears that continued to trickle down from the corners of her eyes.

Jake was sure she wasn't crying about the letter anymore. But he couldn't figure out what the tears were for. Had she realized that they wouldn't have much time left? Was she already contemplating leaving? Or was it something else?

"You should probably check on Sam and Emma before we leave."

"They'll be fine," Jake said.

He held her jacket out for her and as she pulled it on, she looked around the great room. "I really like this place, Jake. It doesn't matter how much you paid for it or how much it will cost to fix it. It was worth every penny."

Caley followed Jake back into town. He pulled into the parking lot of a small Italian restaurant next to the post office downtown and waited for her to pull in next to him. Jake had survived on their take-out pizza when he had visited North Lake in the winter. As they stood at the bar perusing the menu, he glanced at a waitress standing near the end. She smiled at him and gave him a little wave.

"Hey, Jasmine," he murmured as she approached.

"Jake," she said, smiling brightly. "You're back in town."

"My brother's getting married," Jake explained. He turned to Caley. "This is Caley Lambert. My brother is marrying her sister, Emma. She's the maid of honor."

Jasmine nodded. "It's nice to meet you." She turned all her attention back to Jake. "So why didn't you call me when you got in? I still have your jacket at my place. And that fancy corkscrew of yours. You should really come over and pick them up. And bring a bottle of wine along."

Jake had decided to forfeit the jacket and the cork-screw just so he wouldn't have to see Jasmine again. She was one of those women who looked good on first meeting but grew more demanding with each successive date. Jake had dated her for three months, off and on, and when she'd begun talking about kids and marriage, he'd decided to stop.

He'd never had the heart to lead a girl on, to make her believe that he felt something more than he actually did. When it got to that point with Jasmine, he'd stopped calling. But it appeared that she didn't think it was completely over. "What do you want on your pizza?" Jake asked.

"Everything," Caley said. "But no meat."

"Then that's not everything," he said.

"It's all the vegetables," Caley said.

"Are olives vegetables? What about anchovies?"

"No anchovies—anchovies are fish. Green and black olives, green peppers, roasted red peppers, mushrooms and spinach."

Jake wrinkled his nose, then repeated the order to Jasmine. "And then I'd like another pizza with pep-peroni and mushrooms."

"Are you going to eat that here?" Jasmine asked.

"Can you have them deliver it?" Jake asked.

Her smiled dissolved. "Sure. Where to?"

"Northlake Inn. Room 312," Jake said. He pulled out his wallet and handed her enough for the bill and a nice tip, then took Caley's hand and headed back toward the door. Jake could feel Jasmine's eyes on him as they left, but he didn't care. He was with Caley now and, as far as he was concerned, he was off the market.

"So, obviously you two dated."

"We did. Last summer. And into the fall for a while. But she lives here and I was in Chicago, so we didn't see much of each other."

"She seems nice," Caley said.

Jake smiled. "I don't want to see her. I like seeing you."

"But I don't live here."

"Maybe we'll have to find a way to work around that," Jake suggested. He knew he was taking a risk, but it was time for her to know where he stood. He'd grown too attached to Caley to not wonder if she felt the same way.

When they reached the street, Caley turned to him. "Jake, we both know how this is supposed to end. I have a job in New York. I have people who depend on me. I can't move back here. If I did, I'd lose everything I worked so hard to build."

"I know," Jake said, nodding. He glanced down at her hands, her fingers so small and delicate in his. So now he knew. He'd suspected when it came down to choices, she'd choose her life on the East Coast. But the last few days, he'd felt they'd come close to considering a future together. And it was silly to think that she was the one who would have to relocate. He could work out of New York just as easily as Chicago.

But Jake wouldn't make that offer until he knew for sure what the future held. "Why don't you head back to the inn," he said. "I'm going to pick up some beer and a bottle of wine. I'll meet you there."

As he watched her leave, he felt the distance between them growing—not just physically but emotionally. She'd begun to pull away now, as if she were preparing herself to leave. He'd seen her do it time and time again in the past, when she'd been hurt or afraid of her feelings for him. Her offense had always been a stubborn defense, choosing to stand back and shut him out rather than admit she might feel something deeper.

But this time, Jake saw her retreat as a good sign. She was fighting her feelings for him and that must mean that she felt something. It wasn't much to go on, but Jake was satisfied that it was enough.

CALEY MUNCHED ON A PIECE of pizza as she flipped through the channels. She stopped at a *Star Trek* rerun and frowned. She didn't watch much television and she couldn't believe that they were still showing *Star Trek*. The program had to be fifteen years old. "This is still on? Remember how you used to make me watch this? I hated this show."

"You loved this show," Jake said, popping open a can of beer and pointing to the screen.

She shook her head. "No, I didn't. It was too confusing. And that Captain Picard was so…bald."

"Then why did you come over and watch it with me every day?"

Caley picked a mushroom off her pizza, then threw it at him. "Duh. Why do you think? Because I was hoping that one day you might be overcome with desire for me and throw me down on the sofa and kiss me." She took another bite of her pizza. "I had a very active fantasy life."

"Did you ever see us together?" Jake asked.

"All the time," she replied.

"No, I mean together. For good. Forever."

Caley had felt his unease all evening. She sensed he had questions to ask but she'd tried to keep the conversation from getting too serious. In truth, she was as confused today as she had been on the day she arrived back in North Lake. Only, she was confused about different things.

Over the past few days, she'd realized that Jeff Winslow had been right. There was a certain charm to living a small-town life. And she hadn't missed the stress of work at all. The panic attacks that had been plaguing her had disappeared and she was finally sleeping through the night without waking up in a cold sweat, wondering what she might have forgotten to do at work. The only time she felt them return was when her cell phone rang. Like Pavlov's dog, she responded to the sound of the Mozart ditty. She even reprogrammed the ring to see if a new tune might be easier to take. But it didn't matter. The moment she saw a work number come up on the caller ID, she started to get queasy and fluttery and a little woozy.

She'd been happy here with Jake and though she didn't want it to end, Caley knew that, for all practical purposes, a future with him would be difficult. They had both built careers in big cities. Those cities just happened to be seven hundred miles apart. It seemed like a long way. But then, it was only a few hours by plane. She flew back and forth to L.A. at least once a month to see a client there and thought nothing of it.

Conceivably, if she wanted to see him, she could call Jake at lunchtime and be in Chicago by supper. It was possible and with every minute that passed, Caley was thinking more and more about what could be instead of what might have been.

"I should probably go check on Sam and Emma," Jake said. "Do you want to stay here or come with me?"

"I can come with you. I do want to see how Emma is doing. I feel a little guilty leaving her out there all alone. I mean, she's with Sam, but I think she might be pretty angry that we just left them there."

She picked up the pizza box and set it on the table near the window, then turned to Jake. He was stretched out on the bed, wearing just his jeans and boxers. His feet were bare, as was his chest, and he looked so completely at home, as if they'd been together for years and this was just an ordinary night.

"What?" he said, glancing over at her.

"Nothing," Caley said. She grabbed her sweater and tugged it on over her head. Then she looked at him again. Slowly, she crossed the room and ran her hand through his messy hair. "I like this. It doesn't have to be all passion and excitement," she said. "Although I do enjoy that."

"You want passion and excitement?" Jake asked. "I can do that. I just thought you were hungry."

"No," Caley said. "I mean, I love it when we…you know."

"Yeah, I know."

"But this is nice, too. It's comfortable. I've never really had this with a man. It feels real. We can be together and there's no pressure."

"Now you're starting to make me feel bad," Jake teased. "I don't want to be boring."

"You're not."

Jake got to his feet and grabbed his shirt, pulling it on. "You're right. I'm not. Come on, I'll show you some excitement."

"We're not having sex in a public place," Caley warned.

"No. We'll save that for later. I'm going to show you some real small-town fun."

Five minutes later, they pulled on their jackets and were headed back to Jake's car. It had grown colder, the temperature dipping toward the teens, and Caley pulled her hood up around her face. When she got inside the truck, Jake flipped on the heater full blast and then headed down Lake Street to the boat landing.

"Are we going to watch the submarine races?" she asked.

"Nope," he said. "We're going out on the lake."

Caley felt a rush of panic. "In this truck? Oh, no we're not."

"Don't worry. It's safe. The ice is really thick this year. We just have to watch out for ice-fishing holes."

Caley screamed as they drove from the landing onto the ice, expecting the truck to fall through the moment it got over the water. When it didn't, she glanced over at Jake. "Are you sure we're safe?"

Jake turned to her. "I would never do anything to hurt you." He'd expressed the sentiment before but Caley hadn't realized until now how strongly he felt it.

"All right. I taught you how to drive, now I'm going to teach you how to spin doughnuts. In the time-honored tradition of high school drivers, these are things you'll need to know. Number one, turn off the four-wheel drive. Number two, make sure your seat belt is buckled. Number three, don't steer into the skid. Got it?"

"I don't really want to do this," she said.

"It'll be fun," Jake assured her. With that, he hit the accelerator and the truck took off. A moment later, he made a sharp turn and they began to spin on the ice. Caley screamed, clutching at the door handle. At first, she was terrified that they were going to break through at any minute. But as the fear wore off, Caley found that the danger was exhilarating.

When Jake finally pulled the truck to a stop in the middle of the lake, she was breathless, her pulse racing. "That was amazing. Almost better than sex," she said with a giggle.

Jake pulled the truck out of gear and then crawled over the console, pressing Caley up against the door. "I think we ought to make a comparison right here and now. A little experiment."

"You want to have sex in the middle of a frozen lake?"

Jake nodded. "I intend to seduce you in other memorable spots. That way, when you go back home, you won't forget me."

Caley heard the teasing tone in his voice, but the humor didn't extend to his eyes. She reached out and smoothed her palm over his cheek. "I'll never forget this," she murmured. She touched her lips to his and a moment later, they were caught in a passionate kiss.

She felt all the longing and the need between them. But she also felt a bittersweet resignation that from now on, every moment counted. As they slowly began to undress each other, Caley wondered how she'd ever be able to do without this. Passion had never been a big part of her sex life, but now that she'd experienced it with Jake, she couldn't imagine doing without it—or him. Would it even be possible to go a week without touching him or kissing him or feeling him move inside her?

"Are you sure we should be doing this?" she asked, running her fingers through his hair. "If we fall through, they're going to find our frozen bodies in a very compromising position."

Jake worked at the buttons of her blouse. "But at least they'll know we died happy."

"And since we'll be frozen together, they'll have to bury us together."

Jake groaned. "Now that's just morbid."

A loud pop shattered the silence outside the truck and Caley jumped, startled by the sound. "What was that?"

"The ice," Jake said. "It creaks and pops. But it won't break."

Caley struggled to sit up and then rebuttoned her blouse. "Although this would be a lovely little story to tell friends and neighbors, I'm not sure that I'll be able to summon up the needed concentration to truly enjoy myself here."

"You wanna go back?" Jake asked.

"Yes, please," she replied. "If you get me off this ice, then I promise you can have your way with me."

"And if I hum, will you do a striptease?" Jake asked.

Caley thought about his request for a few seconds, then realized there were all kinds of fantasies left for them to explore. "Yes. But then I get to hum and you have to strip."

Jake quickly straightened up and began to put his clothes back in order. Then he got behind the wheel and put the truck back into gear. "Would you like to see how fast we can go on the ice?"

"No," she said.

Jake hit the accelerator and they took off again. "The only thing you have to remember is that it takes a lot longer to stop."

He drove the SUV off the ice at the boat landing in town. When he reached the intersection for East Shore Road, he turned. A few minutes later, they were bumping back down the drive at Havenwoods. Jake jumped out of the truck. "I'll be right back," he said.

As promised, he returned a few minutes later, a smile on his face.

"How were they?" she asked.

"Good, as far as I could see through the window.

I think they might be asleep. I left Sam's cell phone on the porch. If they need it, they'll find it."

Caley nodded, then reached over and furrowed her fingers through the hair at Jake's nape. "Sometimes it feels like we've lived years in these few days. Back when we were kids, everything moved so slowly. And now, I can barely keep up."

"It's because we have a clock ticking," Jake said. He glanced over at her. "You know, we could just shut the clock off. The wedding is scheduled for Thursday night. If it happens, then we're done with our duties. We could grab a couple plane tickets to some warm spot and spend the weekend together. Or the next week, if you can take off work."

The idea was intriguing. Caley had plans to fly back to New York early Friday morning, hoping to have the weekend to catch up on the work she'd missed. But she was the boss now. If she couldn't let a little work slide, then what was the point of being in charge?

"We could do that," Caley said, surprised at how her attitude had changed.

"Mexico?" Jake suggested.

"Or the Caribbean. Someplace warm with pretty beaches and lots of fruity drinks. And luxurious rooms with big bathtubs. And a soft bed covered by one of those mosquito nets."

He grabbed her hand and pressed his lips against

her wrist. "That sounds nice," he said. "Hey, if Sam and Emma don't get married, we could go on their honeymoon."

Caley gave him a disapproving look. "Don't even say that. I want to believe that they'll work things out, don't you?"

Jake nodded. "I know. Me, too. I'll make the plans. We can leave right after the reception."

When they got back to the inn, Jake steered the car into a parking spot behind the building. Then he helped Caley out, grabbing her waist and setting her down in front of him. He kissed her deeply, his hands skimming over her body, searching through the layers of clothes she wore.

"Leave it to fate to put us together in the middle of winter," he muttered as he pulled up her sweater and rubbed his cold hands on her belly. "Too many clothes."

Caley giggled, pushing him away. "I'm sure we'll figure out a way to remedy that." She reached down and threw a handful of snow at his face. "Maybe we should find a vacation spot where they don't require clothes at all."

Jake gasped. "Are you serious?"

She nodded. "Why not? I'd like that, spending my entire day naked instead of bundled up like this."

Jake shook his head. "I don't think so."

"What? Are you a prude? You shouldn't be embarrassed. You're very well represented down there."

Jake chuckled. "Am I?"

Caley nodded. "Yes. Though I haven't a big sample to compare you to, I'd say that most women would find you more than adequate."

"Oh, lovely," he murmured. "More than adequate. That makes me feel good."

"Look at me!" She pointed to her breasts. "I should be the one feeling inferior."

"You have the most beautiful breasts in the world," he said. "I can't imagine how they could be more perfect."

Caley grinned. "So what's the problem then?"

"Oh, there are several I can think of. First of all, if you're running around naked, then I'm going to be running around sporting major wood. That's just a fact. And I don't think the public needs to be seeing that. And I also don't think strange men should be looking at your body the way that I do. I like being the only one to enjoy that pleasure."

"I like your body," Caley said. "And I'd like showing it off to other women."

"How about if I promise to flash an old lady at the airport? Would that satisfy you?"

Caley held out her hand to him. "I suppose it will have to do. And you were the one questioning my daring. You're all talk and no action, Jake."

Jake picked her up and tossed her over his shoulder. "You want action. I'll show you action." He carried her through the lobby, much to the interest of the front-desk clerk. Caley giggled as they stepped onto the elevator and she made Jake turn around so she could push the button for the third floor.

If she wasn't already in love with Jake, then she was falling awfully fast. And right now, Caley had no intentions of doing anything about it.

7

JAKE SKATED IN A SLOW CIRCLE, moving the hockey puck along the ice with his stick. Then, sprinting across the ice, he took a shot at the plastic crate he was using for a goal. The puck popped up and then disappeared into glittering snow just beyond the rink.

He skated to the edge and searched for the puck. When he finally found it, Jake tossed it back onto the ice and plodded through the snow in his skates. Glancing up, he saw Caley standing on the stairs leading down to the lake's shore. He stopped and watched her for a long moment, drawing in a deep breath and letting it go.

He'd barely seen Caley all day and when he'd tried to talk to her at the inn early that afternoon, she'd been preoccupied and irritated. They'd made plans for an early dinner and she promised to meet him at the boathouse. But she was three hours late and Jake ended up eating with his parents and siblings.

Everything had been going so well. Maybe this

was bound to happen. If it was going to come to an end, then better with a bang than a whimper, he thought. Yet, he wasn't willing to concede defeat just yet. He still had two more days, the rehearsal tomorrow and the wedding the next day. He turned away from her and returned to skating, moving around the perimeter of the homemade hockey rink.

"I'm sorry I'm late," Caley shouted.

"No problem."

She watched him skate for a while. "I'd like to explain."

"You want to talk, get a pair of skates and a stick," he said. "I'm playing hockey right now."

"Come on, Jake. Don't be mad. I had to work. There was a big crisis and they needed me on a conference call. Then I had to write up a strategy report and send that in. And I haven't been answering my messages, so my boss had a few choice words to say about the responsibilities of a partner at John Walters."

"Do you even like your job?" Jake asked. He faced her, skating backward, until he reached the edge of the cleared ice. He skidded to a stop and rested his hands on his hockey stick.

"Of course I do."

"Do you?"

"It's a job. I get paid a lot of money. I like the money."

"So, that's what it's all about then?"

"No. I suppose there's some satisfaction in it. Although I spend most of my time making my clients look good when they do bad things. It's not the most noble job on the planet. But I'm good at it. It's what I do."

"Maybe you should try something new," he suggested. He skated toward the goal again and took another shot. This time, the puck hit the inside of the crate and knocked it backward. When he turned back around, Caley was trudging back up to the house.

He skated to the other end of the pond, watching her retreat. He felt an empty ache tighten in his gut and Jake cursed softly. Maybe it had been a little too perfect to last. He'd managed to convince himself that he and Caley had something special, that they were meant for each other. But the more he pushed, the more she drew away. He'd begun to think that maybe there were other reasons why she was so anxious to get back to New York.

"At least I didn't love her," he murmured to himself. "Not the way I could have."

But even as he said the words, Jake knew that they weren't entirely true. What he felt for Caley was more than he'd ever felt for any other woman, more than he could imagine feeling for another. He didn't want to think of the two of them in finite terms, a relationship with a beginning and an end. Caley was the kind of woman who could keep him fascinated for a lifetime, the kind of woman he wanted to love.

Hell, if she was going back to patch things up with her old boyfriend, then he didn't stand much of a chance. Jake drew a sharp breath as a sudden realization struck. Was this her way of evening the score? He'd rejected her years ago and now she'd reject him. It certainly would put her back on top, Jake mused. And that was always the game between them, who could best the other.

Jake continued to skate along the edge of the rink, moving fast enough to make his lungs burn and his heart pound. He turned the notion over in his head, but it was hard to reconcile it with the woman he'd come to know over the past week.

Though Caley might want to balance the scales, she'd done that in many other ways. He had fallen hard and hadn't done much to hide his feelings from her. In truth, he'd done everything in his power to make her see how much he cared.

"Will you talk to me now?"

Jake turned the corner and saw Caley standing at the end of the rink, using a hockey stick to balance herself on her skates.

"Play," he said.

"I can't keep up with you."

"Try," he muttered.

When he came around the rink again, Caley

skated after him, grabbing him around the waist and hanging on until they both fell to the ice. She hit hard, slamming down on her shoulder and crying out in pain. Jake quickly knelt down next to her.

"What the hell are you doing?"

"Trying to talk to you. But you don't want to listen."

Jake helped her sit up and gently rubbed her shoulder. "All right. Talk. What do you want from me? I've pretty much put everything on the line here and for a while, things were good between us. Now it seems that everything is moving backward."

"I don't know what you expect," Caley said. "Until a week ago, I was seeing another man. I'm not sure I'm ready to jump back into a serious relationship, especially with someone who lives halfway across the country."

"It's not halfway," Jake insisted. "It's about a third."

"All right, tell me how it would work, Jake," she said. "How would we do it? Would we spend every weekend together? Or would we see each other once a month? Would we talk on the phone every day? Would you go out with other women? Would I be free to date other men?"

"I don't know," Jake said. "We'd have to figure that all out."

"I had a relationship with a man I never saw," Caley said. "It didn't work. And we lived in the same apartment."

"I'm not him," Jake said.

"I know. But that doesn't make a lot of difference. You still have the capacity to hurt me the same way he did."

Jake turned away, staring off into the distance, fixing his gaze in the direction of Havenwoods as he wondered at the wounds that ran so deep. Was he the cause of her insecurities about men? She was such a confident woman, yet she refused to risk her heart. He'd wounded her so deeply that she was still trying to recover.

Maybe he was the only one who could heal that hurt. Jake took a deep breath. "I'm in love with you," he said, struggling to his feet. He pulled her up beside him, handing her her hockey stick. "Maybe I've always been in love with you. I don't know. But I figured you should probably know. This is the last time I'm going to say it and whatever you decide to do with it, I'll be all right."

She opened her mouth to speak, then forced a smile, as she considered his admission. "I—I don't know what to say," she murmured. "There was a time when that's all I wanted to hear. But back then, it was just a fantasy. Now it's—"

They'd so carefully avoided any talk of the future, choosing to keep their relationship simple, sexual. And now he'd put all his cards on the table. Maybe he'd always known they'd be together. Perhaps that's why he'd turned her down all those years before. Because, deep inside, he knew they'd be together again—they'd have a second chance.

"How do you know you love me?" she asked.

Jake shrugged. "I don't know. I mean, I don't know how. I just feel it."

"Maybe you just need me," she said. "There's a difference, you know."

Jake sucked in a sharp breath, the cold air clearing his head. "No," he murmured. "That's not it." He grabbed her hands. "It's more than that."

"Don't do this," Caley murmured, forcing a smile. "It will only make things difficult in the end."

Jake cursed beneath his breath. "So what? I don't care. Maybe things should be difficult. Maybe it should be hard for us to leave each other. What's so wrong about that? At least I can admit I have feelings for you."

"I can admit that," Caley said. "We've known each other for years. Of course we'd care."

"It's more than that," Jake said.

Caley tugged her hands from his and shoved them in her jacket pockets. "I should get back up to the house. My mother is going crazy trying to figure out what's happening with this wedding."

"And I should go check on Sam and Emma. I'm going to spend the night out at Havenwoods."

"I—I thought we could—"

Jake shook his head. "You're right. We need to step back. I need some space."

She stared at him for a long moment, her expression unreadable. Then she nodded. "I understand. It's all right." Caley turned and skated over to the edge of the ice, then carefully climbed up onto the shore, maneuvering along the small path cut through the snow. When she reached the spot where she'd left her boots, she plopped down and began to unlace her skates.

She slipped her feet into her boots, then stood and hung her skates over her shoulder. "I'll talk to you later," she said.

"Later," he repeated.

It should be easy to rationalize the end of their time together, Jake mused. He'd walked away from any number of women with whom he'd shared longer relationships. But it wasn't just the physical uncoupling that he found difficult. He'd always been attached to Caley emotionally and that bond had strengthened over the past week.

Even now, the thought of letting her go caused an ache deep inside him, an emptiness that couldn't be filled. Maybe this was what he'd done to her all those years ago. He found it impossible to imagine being with another woman. The kind of pleasure that he'd experienced with Caley had been unique and perfect and it would be hard to find with anyone else.

Jake closed his eyes and drew a deep breath of the

chilly night air. He would get over her and he'd learn to live without her. It was just a matter of letting go.

WHEN CALEY ARRIVED at the lake house the next morning for breakfast, the house was noisy with excitement. She walked into the kitchen to find the entire family, including Emma, gathered around the table eating pancakes. Her mother turned to smile at her.

"The wedding is back on," Emma cried, her eyes bright and her smile wide. "We have to go over the final plans with the caterer and then I want to decorate the room we're using for the reception. And you have to pick up your dress and I have to pick up Sam's tux." She jumped out of her chair and threw her arms around Caley's neck. "Thank you," she whispered. "For everything."

Emma glanced around at her family. "I have to go!" she said. "I'll see you all later. I can't believe I'm getting married tomorrow." She hurried out of the room, leaving them all breathless.

Caley breathed a silent sigh of relief. It had worked. She and Jake had managed to fix the mess they'd created. She returned her mother's smile. "I'm so happy for them." She drew a ragged breath. It was almost over, she mused. But she wasn't thinking about the wedding. She was thinking about her time with Jake.

It hit her hard, like a punch to the stomach. Once

the wedding was done, she and Jake would go their separate ways. Though they'd talked about a vacation, Caley knew it wouldn't be the wisest choice for them.

"I'm just going to go get dressed," she said.

"No, sit down and have something to eat," her mother insisted. "You look a little pale."

"I-I'm really not hungry. I'll grab some coffee at the inn. It's going to be a busy day."

She hurried back out of the kitchen and walked to the front door. She hadn't slept more than a few hours last night. Instead, she'd stared at the ceiling and tried to convince herself that she didn't need to drive over to Havenwoods and crawl into bed with Jake. She didn't need to feel his naked body against hers or enjoy the touch of his hands on her skin. She didn't need any of that!

But the more she tried to talk herself out of Jake, the more Caley realized she'd gotten herself so tangled up in him there'd be no way out. She'd done it again, only this time she'd known better. She was an adult and should have been able to control her feelings. But from the moment they'd first made love, she'd been lost.

All her talk about keeping things simple between them had been part of the wall she'd tried to build. But faced with the reality of their situation, that wall had crumbled in front of her. Her body belonged to him, along with her heart and her soul, and Caley knew that was all her fault. She'd fallen in love with Jake all over again, and this time, it was going to hurt a lot worse.

Caley opened the car door and slid inside, then stared out the windshield at the snowy landscape. Tears pressed at the corners of her eyes, but she refused to surrender to them. She had two nights left and if she could bear that, then everything else would get easier. Maybe that was all she needed to set herself back on the right course.

It was the wedding and all that silly romantic stuff that went along with it. That was her problem. She saw Emma and Sam ready to make a lifelong commitment and she felt left behind. After all, she was the elder sister and she should be setting the example, shouldn't she?

Instead, she had opted for lust and passion, instant gratification with no strings attached. They'd shared the best sex she'd ever had and it had left her aching for more. But she'd learned a long time ago that lust wasn't love.

Caley closed her eyes and ran her hands through her hair, trying to recall his touch. He was so gentle, yet there was a silent danger to the way her caressed her, as if he held the key to her body and its pleasure. Only he knew how to make her hunger for his touch, to crave the feel of him inside her.

She groaned and reached for the ignition, letting her hair fall back into her face. "Tell him," she whispered to herself. "Take a chance. Once you say it, maybe it will be true."

It wasn't so hard to imagine them together. They were such good friends that life with Jake would be easy. Loving him could be the most natural thing in the world. She stared at her reflection in the rearview mirror. She'd always run her life with such single-minded determination. And now, she couldn't even make a simple decision about her happiness.

The drive to the inn was quick and uneventful. She was getting used to navigating in the snow and ice now and wasn't afraid to drive a bit faster. When she arrived, she pulled the car into the parking lot and glanced around for Jake's SUV. But it wasn't where she'd hoped it would be. He'd spent the night at Havenwoods—was he still there?

Caley threw the car into Reverse and backed out, then turned toward East Shore Road. She had to trust her feelings and, ultimately, trust him. He wasn't a boy anymore. Jake knew what he wanted. He wanted her.

As she steered down the narrow drive through the trees, Caley felt her nerves begin to get the better of her. But she tried to marshal the same courage she'd found that night of her eighteenth birthday.

Though a long-distance relationship wasn't a

perfect option, they could make it work. Seeing each other once a month was far better than never being together again. There'd be frequent-flier miles and meetings in cities in between New York and Chicago. As long as the passion was there, they could make it work.

When she reached the bottom of the drive, Caley looked around, but didn't see Jake's truck. She hopped out of the rental car, then walked back to the summer kitchen. To her surprise the door was ajar. It creaked as it swung back and Caley stepped inside.

The last embers of a fire still burned in the hearth. Sam and Emma had left a few hours before, but they'd tidied up the place first. The blankets were pulled neatly over the cot and the towels in the bathroom were folded on the rack. Caley closed the door behind her, then wandered through the room, her heart pounding in her chest.

When she reached the bathroom, she stared into the mirror for a long time, noting the color in her cheeks and the nervous look in her eyes. Reaching out, Caley opened the medicine cabinet and scanned the contents.

Though she'd made love to Jake in the most intimate ways possible, she really didn't know much about his day-to-day life. She pulled out his razor and examined it closely, then sniffed at the can of shaving cream, recognizing the scent. A row of aftershave bottles intrigued her and she tested each one until she found her favorite. Caley slipped it into her jacket pocket with a smile.

Wandering back into the main room, Caley stared at the strange collection of things that Jake found important enough to keep—a bird's nest, a huge pine cone, a pretty pink granite stone that had been worn smooth by water. When she sat down at the drafting table, she noticed the bag from the lingerie store sitting beside it.

Caley reached down and opened it. The items he'd purchased were inside, the tags still attached. She shrugged out of her jacket, then stripped out of the rest of her clothes. After she'd pulled on the sexy camisole and little boy shorts, she searched for a mirror. But the only mirror available was in the bathroom.

Caley stood on the toilet and examined the fit, admiring her backside in the tight-fitting panties. Then she jumped down and went back to the fireplace, holding out her hands to the warmth. She'd never noticed the photos propped up on the mantle.

Reaching out, she grabbed one, then realized that it was a photo of her and Jake taken years ago. They both stood on the old raft that had floated just offshore from their beach. Jake's arms were curled up in a strongman pose and Caley was pointing to him with a wide grin on her face. How simple their life had been back then. Love had been so uncomplicated. Why couldn't it still be easy?

The sound of the door creaking startled Caley out of her thoughts. She turned to find Jake standing in the doorway, the cold wind blowing in around him, his arms filled with firewood. He stepped inside and closed the door.

"Wow," he murmured. "I thought these things only happened in my fantasies."

Caley smiled. "Emma didn't use the gift and you can't return underwear, so I was just trying it on."

"I like it," Jake said as he dropped the wood near the fireplace. "Maybe you should take it off and try it on again. Just so I can get the full effect." He crossed the room, then slipped his hands around her waist and dropped a kiss on her lips.

"I think you just want me to get naked," Caley said.

"I could get naked if you don't want to," Jake said. He shrugged out of his jacket, then began to work on the buttons of his shirt.

Caley reached out to stop him. "I came here to talk to you," she said.

"Dressed like that?"

She bent down and picked up her jacket, then slipped into it. Caley sat down on the edge of the cot and patted the spot beside her. But Jake refused her invitation and continued to stare down at her. "Don't do this," he murmured.

"You don't know what I'm going to say," she replied.

"Yes, I do. You're going to tell me that I shouldn't think about the future. That sooner or later we're going to go our separate ways and that I need to accept that fact." He paused and smiled ruefully. "I can deal. When we got into this, we knew that it would end. I'd just rather it end after our vacation than before."

Caley swallowed hard, pushing back the lump of emotion in her throat. That wasn't at all what she was planning to say. She wanted to tell him to give her a chance, to give her time to get over her doubts and fears about commitment. But he was giving up so easily. "You can 'deal'?" she asked.

Jake shrugged. "You were right, Caley. I got all caught up in this. I should have seen it for what it really was, just an affair. A good time. I know that now. If we try to force it, we'll both end up unhappy and full of regrets.

Caley swallowed hard, trying to keep the emotion from clogging her throat. "That's exactly what I was going to say," she murmured. "I'm glad we're both on the same page."

That was it, then, Caley mused, ignoring the urge to confess her true feelings. She wasn't a teenager anymore and blurting out her love for him would have only caused more problems than it solved. This time, she'd made the right decision. If she'd learned anything in the past eleven years it was that she couldn't make Jake do or be or feel anything that he didn't want to.

Caley looked at him, her gaze taking in the features that had become so familiar to her...and so dear. For a long time, she'd carried an image of him as a twenty-year-old, but now that she'd come to know the man, she could accept him for who he really was.

"I should get dressed," she murmured. "Emma needs some help with the wedding arrangements."

"She and Sam are fine," Jake said. "You know there's a fresh bottle of chocolate syrup over there."

She knew what he was asking, but Caley wasn't sure she ought to agree. He wanted her, needed her body, just one more time. And though she didn't want to admit it, she needed him, too. "Are you planning to make me a cup of hot cocoa? Or a hot-fudge sundae?"

"Yes, I'm planning on making *you* a hot-fudge sundae," he said.

"We don't have any ice cream," Caley said.

"Where we're going, we don't need ice cream." Jake turned and retrieved the bottle of chocolate syrup from the table, then held up the can of whipped cream. "If you don't want to get your new underwear all sticky, I'd suggest you take it off."

Caley crossed the room and grabbed the can of whipped cream from his hand, then tossed aside the cap. She reached up and applied a thin stripe of it to his lower lip. "You're the one wearing too many clothes." Pushing up on her toes, she licked the sweet cream off with the tip of her tongue.

Jake groaned softly. "Maybe this was a mistake."

Caley sprayed a bit of whipped cream on his chin and proceeded to lick it off. She'd make him remember the last days he spent with her. From now on, every minute would be one that he'd recall again and again when he was alone, memories that would stir his desire and make him ache with need. He'd never find another woman who could arouse him the way she could and he'd always be left wondering if he'd made the right choice in letting her go.

Grabbing his hand, Caley placed a dot of cream on each fingertip, then slowly sucked it off, drawing his finger in and out of her mouth playfully. "Would you like to try?" she asked, holding out the can to him.

Jake sprayed a line from her shoulder to her wrist. With exquisite ease, he worked his way up until he pressed a kiss beneath her ear. And then, as if he'd already tired of the game, he tossed the can aside, grabbed her waist and picked her up off her feet. Wrapping her legs around his hips, he kissed her mouth, his tongue tangling with hers, the sweet taste of the whipped cream passing between them.

He carried her to the cot near the fireplace and sat down, Caley on his lap. For a long time, they kissed, exploring each other's mouths until they'd perfected their kisses.

If she could spend the rest of her life kissing Jake, Caley knew it would never become routine. Every kiss sparked her passion and elevated her need until she was frantic for a more intimate connection. But she wouldn't have the rest of her life. She'd have today and tomorrow and that was all.

She slowly undressed him and then drew him back down on the narrow cot, his body sinking down on top of hers, his hips settling between her legs. But as he brought her closer and closer to her release, Caley realized that what they were doing was wrong.

They were both trying to act as if it were just passion and lust driving them forward, as if what they were doing was sex and nothing more. But she knew it wasn't true. The emotional connection was still there, the force that had brought them together in the first place. No matter how much they both tried to ignore it, it wasn't going to go away.

And when it was over and she lay sated in his arms, Caley knew that they hadn't had sex. They'd made love.

8

JAKE STARED AT CALEY across the vestibule of the church. She stood next to Emma, standing so still and quiet that Jake wondered what was going through her mind.

He knew what was going through his. Images of her naked body, arching beneath him in pleasure, her face filled with the rapture of her release, her lips swollen from his kisses. They'd spent three hours making love that afternoon and it still hadn't seemed like enough.

In bed, Caley was adventurous and uninhibited, driven by her desire until he had no choice but to be swept along. The way she touched him was so tantalizing that it made him hard just thinking about it. In just a week she'd come to know his body so well that she could sense his pleasure before he fully felt it.

She glanced over at him and smiled and he licked his bottom lip. A pretty blush stained her cheeks and Jake felt a bit sinful trying to tempt her in church.

But at this point, he was willing to take any opportunity offered.

He listened distractedly as Emma went over the directions for the processional. Jake had never been a best man and was surprised that his future sister-in-law knew so much about the mechanics of a wedding. When she told him to stand at the front of the church next to Sam, he dutifully followed orders and walked down the side aisle, having no idea what his next instruction would be.

A few minutes later, the organ started playing and Caley began her march toward the altar, her hands folded in front of her. He held his breath as their gazes locked and a flood of emotion passed between them. Suddenly, he felt as if this was his wedding and she was walking to him.

Jake looked away, unable to control his feelings. He'd never put much stock in the whole idea of *happily ever after.* But he needed to believe it was possible. If there was one woman who could make him happy for the rest of his life, it had to be Caley. There was no other choice for him.

Desire was a powerful narcotic, a drug that could muddle a man's brain. But this wasn't about desire. He would feel the same in a week or a month or lifetime from now. He knew that in his heart and yet she couldn't see it.

As Caley reached the front of the church, Jake

noticed an odd expression on her face, as if she were about to be sick. Dark circles smudged the skin beneath her eyes and she seemed to be breathing in quick little gasps. When her knees nearly buckled, Jake moved to her side and took her arm.

"No!" Emma corrected from the back of the church. "You stay in that spot next to Sam. You don't take her arm until the recessional."

"Are you all right?" he asked softly.

Caley shook her head. "I-I'm a little dizzy."

"Can we take a break?" Jake asked. "I have to use the bathroom."

"And I—I need to get a drink of water. I'm—thirsty. Excuse me." Caley shoved her little ribbon bouquet into the minister's hands, then headed for the door. Jake followed her, ignoring the curious glances of their parents.

When she reached the vestibule, she shoved the front door open and stepped out into the cold. Bending over at the waist, Caley drew a deep breath and let it go, her sigh visible in the freezing temperatures.

Jake put his hand on her back and slowly rubbed. "Are you going to be sick?"

"I—I don't know," she said.

"Tell me if you are because I'm really no good with that. If I see you get sick, then I'll get sick. And I don't want them to find us out here puking on each other's shoes." That brought a small giggle and Jake was pleased that he'd been able to distract her. "What's wrong?"

"Nothing," Caley said, waving him away. "My stomach is just all tied up."

"Because of the wedding?"

She glanced up at him. "I get these panic attacks. I haven't had one lately and this one is really bad. Everything is happening so fast. I haven't had time to think. I just need some time to think."

"Caley, you do realize that we're not the ones getting married here, don't you? That's Sam and Emma. The best man and maid of honor aren't supposed to get cold feet before the wedding."

She slowly straightened, taking another deep breath. "I'm sorry."

Jake noticed the damp on her cheeks, then realized she was crying. He reached up and brushed a tear away with his thumb. "What's wrong? Tell me."

"I'm tired," she said. "And a little emotional. Emma is getting married. She's all grown-up and moving forward with her life and I feel like I don't have any idea where I'm going."

"What do you want, Caley?" He heard the frustration in his voice, but Jake couldn't help himself. Why couldn't she realize how rare it was to find something as special as what they shared?

"I don't know. I just don't want to feel like this, all confused and uncertain. I want my life to make sense. And it used to, a long time ago." She stared up at him. "I was happy once. I know I was."

"And you're not happy now?"

"No!" She paused. "Yes! Maybe."

"Which is it?"

"We've had a wonderful week together. I've had a chance to live out a teenage fantasy. And that should be enough."

Jake knew there was something more she had to say. "What do you want?" he repeated.

A weak smile curled the corners of her mouth and she took another deep breath. "I want you to tell me to stop being such a baby," she said. Caley ran her fingers through her hair and pasted a calm expression her face. "Sorry. I haven't been getting a lot of sleep lately. It's hard to survive on sex and whipped cream alone."

"We've been giving it a valiant try, though," Jake murmured.

"I could have used that vacation," she said.

"We can still go. You just say the word and I'll take you away from all this."

"I know you would."

"Come on," Jake said. "Let's go back in and do our duties and then we'll have dinner with the family and go back to Havenwoods. I'll make a big fire and we'll curl up on the cot and just sleep."

She looked up at him through damp eyes. "I can't. I promised Emma that I'd stay with her tonight at the inn."

"Then maybe we'll both get some sleep," he said. Jake took her hand and tucked it in the crook of his arm and led her back inside the church. Emma was waiting to walk up the aisle again and she waved Caley over. Jake gave her fingers a squeeze, then let her go before he moved up the side aisle to stand next to Sam.

"What is going on with you two?" Sam asked.

"Nothing," Jake said. "She just got a little emotional waiting for Emma to come up the aisle. It's a sister thing."

"Are you sure?" his brother prodded.

Jake nodded. He was sure. It was nothing.

This time, as Caley did her march, he grinned at her, trying to lighten her mood. She was right. They hadn't had much sleep and with everything they'd done over the past six days, it was a wonder one of them hadn't gone round the bend. It was also a testament to how well they got along.

"The perfect woman," Jake murmured.

"What?" Sam said, glancing over his shoulder.

"She's the perfect woman. Emma. Don't you think?"

Sam smiled and nodded. "Yeah, for me she is."

"And when you find the perfect woman, you don't let her go," Jake continued.

Sam frowned at him. "I'm marrying her."

The rest of the rehearsal passed without a hitch. Jake listened carefully to the directions that the minister gave him, but his mind was occupied with thoughts that he wasn't sure he ought to be having. He *could* get Caley to stay, to live here with him. All he had to do was ask her to marry him. She'd have to believe he loved her if he did that.

But though the plan sounded simple, Jake knew it was filled with danger. What if she said no? He almost preferred not knowing how she felt to knowing that she didn't want him. He thought back to her offer on the beach that night. How much courage had it taken her to approach him, her emotions laid bare? Couldn't he summon the same courage for her?

When all the details had been worked out for the service, Sam and Emma walked back down the aisle, Emma clutching her bouquet of ribbons and looking like a radiant bride. Jake and Caley met at the head of the aisle and he took her hand again and walked with her to the back of the church.

The family gathered again in the vestibule before splitting up to drive to the restaurant for the rehearsal dinner. Jake waited around until nearly everyone had left before cornering Caley in the shadows of a stairway. "I have to see you tonight," he murmured, raking his fingers through her thick hair.

"I can't. I promised Emma."

"I'll wait in your room at the inn. As soon as she's asleep, meet me."

"What if she wakes up? Or what if she never goes to sleep?"

"I don't want to spend a night without you," Jake said. "That's going to happen soon enough. It doesn't have to happen now, when we're in the same town."

He hadn't realized until now how strong his need was. He'd do anything to be with her—anything. And he'd ask her to stay, even if it meant getting rejected. The risk was well worth the reward.

Jake had to believe Caley just hadn't figured it all out yet. She was still fighting her feelings and when she finally reconciled herself to the fact that she might be in love with him, too, then everything would be clear. There was only one thing standing in their way, Jake mused, and that was their physical relationship.

Sex gave Caley an excuse to think of them in only those terms—lust and release, naked bodies lost in incredible pleasure. The kind of desire they shared would distract anyone—including him. He had to try a different approach. And for that to work, he'd have to keep his clothes on and his hands off her body.

JAKE GLANCED AT HIS WATCH, squinting in the dim light from the lamp beside the bed. He'd assumed

Emma would be so exhausted after the rehearsal dinner and the six glasses of champagne she'd downed that she'd nod off well before midnight. But it was nearly two a.m. and still no sign of Caley. He looked over at the phone, wondering if he ought to call. But she knew he was waiting.

He closed his eyes for just a moment, letting himself relax. She'd been right. They hadn't had much sleep over the past week and it was starting to take its toll. He drew a deep breath and then another; sleep was inevitable.

When he woke up, Jake wasn't sure how much time had passed. But the bedside lamp had been turned off and there was someone in bed beside him. She'd unbuttoned his shirt and unzipped his khakis and was slowly kissing her way down to his belly.

"Caley?" he murmured.

"Were you expecting someone else?"

Jake chuckled as she slid her hand beneath the waistband of his boxers. "No," he said. "You're the one who always crawls into the wrong bed."

"Maybe it was the right bed all along," she whispered.

She took his shaft in her hand and slowly began to stroke, her tongue teasing at the tip of his cock. He was already so hard, but he couldn't recall getting that way. He remembered that he'd wanted to talk, but it was already too late for that. Closing his eyes,

Jake gave himself over to the pleasures she offered. They could talk later, he thought as her warm mouth surrounded him.

Each sensation was heightened, made more intense by the lack of light around them. She'd already removed her own clothes, and he slid his hands over her silken limbs, recognizing each curve and swell of flesh that her body offered. Even in the dark, she was the most beautiful woman he'd ever known.

Slowly, she pushed aside his clothes to kiss and caress him. His shoulders, his nipples and the trail of hair that led down to his erection, it was all hers to enjoy and Jake didn't try to stop her. Caley was intent on seducing him and he wasn't about to question her motives.

As she worked her way over his body, Jake let the desire wash over him in waves. Though he wasn't trying to exert any kind of control, she seemed to sense when he was close to losing it and she slowed her seduction for just a moment.

Her lips continued to return to his shaft again and again, edging him closer to release and then leaving him just shy of orgasm. He'd never ceded so much control to her, but Caley seemed to need it tonight. There was a quiet desperation to her lovemaking. Whenever he made a move to touch her, she gently drew his hand from the damp spot between her legs.

And in the end, Jake didn't fight her. He gave her exactly what she wanted—his body.

Yet as she sank down on top of him, Jake wondered if she'd take more. Did she want his soul and his heart and the rest of his life? If he offered, would she accept? He needed to believe that this feeling would never end, that he'd have eternity to explore it and enjoy it.

But Jake also knew that love could be fickle and fleeting, and even if they stayed together now, they might not be together later. He was willing to try, willing to give her whatever she needed to make it work.

He reached up and cupped her face in his hands, drawing her down into a long, deep kiss, tasting her sweet mouth. He couldn't seem to get enough and when she tried to pull away, Jake held tight, refusing to let her go.

He'd never felt this way before, this frantic need to possess a woman. Where did it come from? Why was it so important for him to claim her? She was his, whether she cared to admit it or not. Her body belonged to him. No man could make her ache the way that he could.

"I love you," he murmured against her lips.

The words came so naturally now, without even a second thought, that Jake knew they were real and not just imagined. He couldn't regret saying them. He did love Caley and nothing would change that.

"I love you, too," she said.

At that moment, Jake knew it would be all right. It may take weeks or months, but there would come a day that she would believe in what she felt. Grabbing her waist, he rolled her over on the wide bed and pulled her legs up alongside his hips. He began to move, slowly at first, his arms braced on either side of her head. He knew exactly how to make her come without his touch and with every other stroke, he withdrew and rubbed against her sex.

Her breathing grew shallow and quick and she moaned softly, grasping at his hips with her hands, raking her nails over his buttocks. He was close to his own release, but Jake ignored the signs and waited for Caley. Their coupling grew in intensity and became wild and uncontrolled. They spoke to each other in ragged fragments, the words disappearing into the darkness as they both lost touch with reality.

And then she was there, arching beneath him and crying out his name. Jake felt her convulse around him and then dissolve into powerful shudders. He let himself go, tumbling over the edge in a free fall of pleasure. He drove into her again and again, burying himself to the hilt until he was completely spent.

Jake had thought he knew what they were together, but suddenly, they'd broken through a wall and reached an entirely different level of pleasure.

He hadn't been driven solely by physical desire this time. Their bodies had touched in the most intimate fashion possible, but this time, so had their souls.

Jake lay down beside her, pulling Caley into the curve of his body and slipping his leg between hers. "I meant what I said," he whispered. "I do love you."

"I know. And I love you."

A long silence grew between them and Jake knew there was more to say. "What does that mean?"

Caley snuggled closer and kissed his chest. "I don't know."

He could sense the bittersweet emotion in her words. Jake reached over and turned on the bedside lamp, determined to look into her face as they spoke. Her eyes were wide, watching him warily. "It has to mean something, Caley. I've never said those words to a woman before and I'm pretty certain you're the last woman I'll say them to."

"Jake, we've known each other for a week."

"We've known each other our whole lives," he countered.

"But that doesn't count."

Jake laughed sharply. "Why the hell not? It should count for a lot. You know me, Caley, and you know that I'll do everything in my power to make this work."

Jake rolled out of bed and snatched up his jeans, then pulled them on. It was difficult enough talking about such serious matters; he wasn't about to do it naked. "I'm not going to push you. If you want me, you know where to find me."

Caley sat up, pulling the bedcovers up around her naked body. Jake watched her, waiting for a reply, some sign that she was thinking about what this meant. "I'm leaving tomorrow right after the wedding reception. I got a call from the office and they need me back in New York on Friday morning. We have a client presentation that got moved up in the schedule and I have to be there to help prepare."

"You don't have to go," Jake said. "You can stay with me. I'll take care of you."

"Don't do this. Don't make me choose. People are depending on me. I can't take that lightly."

"And what about you? Don't you deserve something for yourself?"

In the end, Jake knew she wouldn't change her mind. She wasn't ready. But he also knew there would be another time. What had happened between them couldn't be put aside. Sooner or later, Caley would realize what they'd had and she'd come back to him.

"You should probably get back to Emma," he said. "You wouldn't want her to wake up and wonder where you are." He raked his hand through his hair. "I guess this is goodbye." He smiled and shook his head. "Goodbye, Caley. It's been fun."

"It has," Caley replied.

Jake nodded, fighting the urge to drag her into his arms and kiss some sense into her. But instead he walked to the door and opened it. He looked back once to see her still sitting on the bed, her gaze fixed on him. Then he stepped into the hallway, into a life without her.

He stood, staring at the closed door, for a long time, wondering whether this truly was the end. He'd always thought falling in love was supposed to solve every problem. Instead, it had just compounded the confusion.

He had to believe, to have faith in what he knew to be true. She loved him. And she couldn't live without him.

9

THE PHOTOS of Sam and Emma's wedding had arrived in yesterday's mail but Caley hadn't the courage to open them. She'd tossed them into her bag as she'd left her apartment that morning and now they sat on her desk, inside their padded manila envelope.

She knew what she'd find—happy pictures with smiling faces, everyone looking as if they were having the time of their lives at the wedding and the reception. She thought back to that night. Though it had been a beautiful, romantic wedding, it had also been one of the worst nights of her life, even worse than the night that Jake had turned down her offer.

After making love to Jake, Caley had returned to Emma's room and crawled into bed, determined to finally get a few hours' sleep. But instead she'd stared at the ceiling, thinking about what had passed between them.

The words had changed everything. The first time he'd said them, she'd brushed them off as an expression of his affection. But the second time, it had been more. It had been a promise, one she wanted desperately to return.

Until that moment, Caley had tried to put their relationship in its proper perspective. It had been just a momentary fling, an affair that had a beginning and end. But then Jake had to mess it all up. And worse yet was what she'd done in returning the sentiment. Now it was just dangling out there, unresolved.

She'd finally found a way to close the books on that night eleven years ago. She'd had sex with Jake, it had been wonderful. That part of her life could now be forgotten.

"Closure," she murmured, picking up the envelope. That's all she'd ever expected to get. But now, she'd have to put closure on her closure. Their affair hadn't been an ending but a whole new beginning. Caley had found herself imagining a future with him. Not just a weekend here or there, or a vacation together when they both had time. She'd thought about something permanent, something that might last a lifetime. The only way to get closure on that was to marry Jake.

Caley carefully opened the envelope and set the stack of photos in front of her. Three months had passed, but she could recall every moment of that week as if it were yesterday. There were nights when she lay in bed imagining Jake beside her…above her…inside her. She wondered if he was thinking about her, too, caught up in an arousing dream.

She'd reached for the phone countless times, ready to call him and put an end to the silence. But then, she'd remember his behavior at the wedding—polite, aloof yet properly attentive. He was giving her an out and she'd been a coward and taken it.

Caley flipped through the pictures until she found a photo of her and Emma, sitting at a table. Jake was standing nearby, looking at them both, a tiny smile curling his lips. She found another photo where he was watching her and then another. Caley hadn't realized, but in nearly every photo he was looking at her with an odd expression of…what was it?

She shook her head and set the photos down, then glanced over at a photo of her parents that she kept on her desk. There it was. The same expression on her father's face. He was sitting next to her mother at a picnic and she was smiling at the camera and he was smiling at her. It was love, adoration and respect all mixed into one simple look.

Caley took a deep breath and turned back to her computer screen, the media release blurring in front of her eyes. She'd been working on the copy for the entire day and had only managed to put together the first paragraph. It was due by the end of the day and she couldn't seem to come up with a creative way to announce the merger of two newspapers.

"Who cares?" she murmured to herself, sliding her mouse over the paragraph to delete it. "Yes, people are going to be upset because they'll only have one newspaper instead of two. But they'll get over it. A few months from now, no one will care."

Since the moment she'd arrived back in New York, she'd had a very difficult time settling into work. She'd become increasingly annoyed by what she was asked to do, her boss acting as if the world would end if the public didn't know that the French fries at a popular fast-food restaurant were made with a new blend of spices.

She delegated everything she could to her assistants and spent her day browsing the online real-estate ads in Chicago. She wasn't sure why, but it seemed to make her feel as if she were accomplishing something. She'd also taken to flipping through some old photos she'd found from her childhood, trying to piece together when it was she'd fallen in love with Jake.

Caley reached up and fingered the arrowhead necklace she wore. She'd felt silly putting it on again after all these years, but it was something else that made her feel better, that gave her a measure of contentment.

Summer was approaching and the ice would be gone on the lake. The trees would be green and the shallows would soon be warm enough to swim in. As if by instinct, she started to get that trembling feeling of anticipation, the same feeling she'd had as a teenager. The entire summer seemed to stretch out in front of her, filled with excitement and promise. Filled with Jake Burton.

So why not go home? She could afford to take another week once she got this project done. Jake would most likely be there, working on Haven-woods. She'd fantasized about the moment they'd see each other again. And in every one of her fantasies, they'd fall into each other's arms and the world would suddenly make sense.

Caley had used her job as an excuse all along. In truth, it had been something to hide behind, a convenient reason to avoid commitment. Her career didn't matter anymore. If she wanted to work, she could find a job anywhere. She was talented and intelligent and knew the public relations business better than ninety percent of her peers.

Why not just do it? She could walk into John Walters's office right now and quit. She could clean out her desk, take a cab home and pack up her things. In less than a day, she could make a complete turn in her life and start all over. There had been a time when a thought like that would have terrified her. But now, the idea was infinitely appealing.

The buzzer on her intercom rang, startling her out of her thoughts. She picked up her phone. "Yes?" she said.

"Caley? There's someone here to see you."

"Who is it?" Caley asked.

"I'm not supposed to say," her assistant replied. "It's a surprise. Can I send him in?"

"Him?" Caley swallowed hard.

"Him. Tall, dark and handsome. Says he's related to you."

"Kind of a crooked smile? Pale blue eyes?"

"That's right, Miss Lambert."

She drew a quick breath. "Give me two minutes, then send him in."

Caley jumped up from her desk and grabbed her purse, then hurried to the mirror on the back of her office door. This wasn't how this was supposed to happen! She needed more time, a different haircut, a prettier dress, nicer underwear.

Jake had mentioned that he sometimes got out to the East Coast on business. But why wouldn't he have called first? Caley grabbed her lipstick and dabbed it sparingly on her lips. No need to look too obvious. Maybe he was afraid she'd refuse to see him. She pulled the rubber band out of her hair, then moaned. She hadn't been sleeping well lately, which meant she usually did the minimum to get ready for work in the morning. Oh God, what was she going to say to him? Would he kiss her? Or would it be uncomfortable between them?

A knock sounded on the door and Caley jumped

back, dropping her lipstick in front of her. She quickly kicked it aside, then tossed her purse onto a nearby chair. "All right," she whispered. "I can do this. He doesn't know I've been thinking about him for the past three months. For all he knows, I've moved on."

She reached for the door, steeling herself for the impact of that first glance. Caley wasn't so silly as to think it would be anything but devastating. But when she opened the door, a flood of disappointment washed over her.

"Sam," she said, forcing a smile.

Jake's brother grinned at her and held up his hands. "Surprised?"

"Of course. What are you doing here?"

"I'm on my way to see Emma in Boston. I've got a law school interview at Columbia."

"Law school? Here in New York?"

"I thought, since I was here, I'd stop and see my favorite sister-in-law." He stepped inside, taking in the luxury of her office. "Nice digs. So this is what a partner's office looks like. Maybe I should consider PR instead of law."

"It's all for show," Caley said.

Her gaze fixed on him as he walked around the office. Caley hadn't realized until this very moment how much Sam looked like Jake. Just staring at him made her ache for the sight of Jake's face, for the warmth of his smile and the teasing humor that sparkled in his eyes. She shook herself out of her thoughts and stepped back from the door. "Sit down."

"I thought we might go out for some dinner," Sam suggested as he glanced at his watch. "It's nearly seven. Aren't you hungry?"

"I have this project that we have to get done and people are in and out with questions. I really can't leave. But stay awhile and talk. I'll have my assistant go out and get us some sandwiches." She paused and smiled at Sam as he sat down. "You seem so grown-up with that suit on. All settled and married."

He held up his hand with the wedding ring. "Thanks to you and Jake," Sam said. "If it hadn't been for you two, I'm not sure we would have made it through the first three months of marriage."

Caley felt a blush rise on her cheeks. "How can you say that? We almost ruined your wedding."

"You did us a favor. Emma and I were going into it all naive and wide-eyed. You made us stop and think about what we were doing. You were better than any marriage counselors we could have seen."

"You're only saying that because everything turned out right."

Sam stretched his legs out in front of him and linked his hands behind his head. "Aren't you going to ask me?" he finally said.

"I'm sorry," Caley murmured. "How is Emma?"

"Not Emma," Sam said, meeting her gaze. "Jake. Aren't you going to ask me about Jake?"

"All right. How is Jake?"

"Not so great since you left," Sam said. "He misses you."

"I miss him," Caley admitted. "We're good friends. And it was nice to see him again after such a long time apart."

"You're more than good friends," Sam said.

"What do you mean?"

"Jake and I got drunk one night watching a Bulls game and he told me everything."

"Everything?"

"Can I give you some advice?" Sam asked. "I mean, you don't have to take it. You know what you want more than I do. But I think you and Jake belong together. It's always been that way. You're like a team. You're the reason why Emma and I fell in love."

"How is that?"

"We used to watch you two and you always had such a great friendship. You were equals. We both wanted something like that and when we started dating, we found it." He paused. "Plus, Emma was really hot. Oh, and smart and funny, too. But it was the friendship that sealed the deal. A relationship like that takes years to build and you two already have it. You're ahead of the game."

"But friendship doesn't always turn into love."

"Jake loves you," Sam said. "And I think you love him. And you're both letting it slip away."

"I'm not."

"Caley, I know my brother. And I know the only person who is going to make him happy is you. If you don't feel the same way about him, then you have to tell him straight out so he can get on with his life."

"I do love him."

"I'm throwing a graduation party for Emma on Memorial Day weekend. I'm inviting you and I expect you to come. Jake is going to be there. Maybe you two can…talk." Sam stood up and smiled. "That's really all I came to say. Dinner was just an excuse. So, how far is Chinatown from here?"

Caley walked Sam to the elevator and gave him a hug before sending him on his way with a list of recommendations for his evening in Manhattan. Though she thought about going with him, it was difficult to look at Sam and not think about Jake.

When she returned to the office, she sat down in her chair and reached for her calendar. She had two weeks to decide whether to go home for Emma's party or to put her relationship with Jake permanently behind her. A few days, if she hoped to get a decent airfare.

She reached for the phone and punched in the three-digit number to reach John Walters's assistant. There were other decisions to be made, as well, decisions that would be much more difficult than which flight to take to Chicago. "Alice Ann? It's Caley. Is he still in?" She drew a shaky breath. "I need to see him. I'll be right down."

Caley stared at the phone for a long time, her hand resting on the receiver. She was contemplating changing the course of her life—and all for a man. Was she really ready to do this? Or was she still trying to fulfill some stupid schoolgirl fantasy?

She glanced down at the photos and smiled. "For a man who loves me," she said.

JAKE STOOD IN THIGH-HIGH WATER, near the rotting pier at Havenwoods. "It's got to be at least fifty years old," he shouted to Sam.

"How can you tell?"

"It looks old." He stared down at the rusted motorcycle submerged in three feet of water. Jake had decided to start work on the beach so that he could at least swim when the weather turned hot. But there was so much trash in the lake that he had to do a major cleanup first.

"Can you get your truck down here?" Sam asked. "Maybe you can drag it out."

Jake raked his hand through his hair and stared up at the shore. "No. Maybe we can winch it out. Once we get it on shore, we can probably break it apart. It's pretty rusted."

"Or we can bring Dad's boat over and we can tow it out into the center of the lake."

Jake gave Sam a disapproving look. "That would not be very environmentally sound."

"But it would be easy," Sam countered.

"Go up to the summer kitchen and get that rope that I bought. We'll try to drag it closer to shore and then lift it out."

Jake stared down at the water, then bent over and tried to dig the back wheel out of the mud and sand with his hands. But he couldn't reach without going under. Grabbing a deep breath, he ducked his head beneath the surface and began to tug on the back wheel.

When he ran out of breath, he popped out of the water, shoving his hair out of his face. He looked up on shore for Sam, but instead, saw someone else walking down the path. "Emma," he murmured, wondering how much she'd be able to help.

Over the past few months since Caley had left, he'd been reminded of her on a fairly regular basis each time he'd seen Emma. Emma laughed like Caley, she moved like Caley, she even looked a bit like her older sister, especially in the eyes and around the mouth. Jake had caught himself staring on occasion, picking out that one feature that brought back all the memories of Caley.

He'd done his best to forget her, to move on with his life. But Emma was a constant reminder. This was what he'd have to look forward to for the entire summer, and at Thanksgiving and Christmas and every other major holiday that the Burtons and the Lamberts would now spend together.

Jake knew he ought to be grateful that Caley would probably choose to stay in New York, though he expected he'd probably have to face her once or twice at Christmas. That was nearly seven months away. By that time, he ought to be able to see her without lapsing into some intense sexual fantasy involving condiments.

"Emma, tell Sam to hurry up. I'm not going to stand in this water all day waiting for him."

Emma stood on the shore, her hand shading her eyes, watching him. Her hair was pulled back, but when she turned, he saw a glint of auburn and a curly ponytail. Jake's breath caught in his throat. "Caley?" he called.

She took another step closer and in that moment, he knew it was her. Hell, he'd wondered exactly how he'd feel the next time he saw her and now he knew. His reaction was powerful, like a punch to the stomach, and he could barely grab a breath.

As she walked closer, he could see her face. Her gaze watched him warily and Jake realized that she was as nervous as he was. It had only been three months, time that had crawled by at a snail's pace. But now, it seemed as if time had stopped dead in its tracks. Jake reminded himself to breathe, then waded slowly to the shore.

"I'm here for Emma's party," Caley said.

Jake took some satisfaction that their meeting was affecting her as strongly as him, that she couldn't think of anything more interesting to say. "I figured that."

"I thought it would be better if we saw each other first. I—I didn't want to surprise you and just—be there."

He nodded, his gaze skimming along her beautiful body. He felt a pulsing warmth rush through his bloodstream and pool in his lap. He hadn't had sex since she'd left and for the first time in three months, he felt it. Thankfully, he was wearing baggy board shorts that hid his reaction. "Good idea," Jake murmured. "So, how have you been?"

"Good," Caley said. "Busy. I've meant to call but…"

He waited for a long moment, wondering if she planned to finish the thought. When she didn't, he gave it a try. "But you were stranded on the top of a mountain without a phone? But you were in the hospital unconscious in a coma? Or you were on assignment for the CIA? Because that's where I was."

A tiny smile quirked the corners of her lips. "But I wasn't sure what I wanted to say," Caley finished. "I'm still not sure."

"You could tell me that you missed me," Jake suggested. "That would be a start."

"All right. I missed you. A lot."

Jake took that as his cue and he stepped out of the water and walked up to her spot on the shore. "When two people meet after being away for a long time, they usually kiss. Especially if they've missed each other. It's kind of a tradition, I guess." He leaned forward and brushed his mouth against hers.

He'd intended the kiss to be simple, almost platonic. But the moment their mouths touched, a current of desire passed between them. It was as palpable as heat lightning on a humid summer night, startling and intense.

Jake grabbed her waist and pulled her against him, kissing her again, this time more deeply. She immediately opened to his assault, as if she were desperate to taste him, too.

His hands skimmed over her body, feeling the familiar curves. She was dressed in a thin cotton shirt and a skirt that hugged her hips and her backside and it wasn't difficult to imagine her body beneath, all soft skin and naked flesh. Without speaking, he grabbed her hand and drew her along to the summer kitchen, the two of them climbing the rise from the water's edge to the cabin.

When they got inside, Jake walked to the bathroom and grabbed a towel, drying his hair and chest. Then, he kicked off his wet shoes and rinsed his feet in the tub. She was standing in the middle of the room when he returned, looking even more beautiful than he'd remembered.

"It's strange," he said. "I feel like I used to on that first day of summer vacation, when I'd see you after all that time apart. I was never sure of what I should say. Every summer, I'd spend hours thinking of a clever opening line."

"You should have tried kissing me," Caley murmured.

"I can see that now." Jake walked across the room and slipped his hands around her waist. "How have you been? And don't tell me about work."

"I've been…confused," Caley said. "I guess that's the best word for it. But I've begun to simplify my life."

"I've missed you, Caley. I'm not afraid to admit that."

"I'm glad," she murmured. With a trembling hand, she reached out and smoothed her palm over his chest. Her fingers raked through the trail of hair between his collarbone and his belly and Jake closed his eyes and enjoyed the feel of her touch.

He wanted to strip off her clothes and take her to bed, to prove that the desire they'd once shared still pulsed between them. Jake gazed into her eyes, knowing that she couldn't refuse him. But sex, however pleasurable between them, wouldn't solve their problems. They had to find a way to be together, and not just physically.

"How long are you staying?"

Caley shrugged. "I haven't decided. I wasn't sure how things would go." She took a ragged breath. "I need to be back by Thursday. So, five or six days."

"We can get into a lot of trouble in five or six days," he said.

"If we want to get in trouble," Caley replied. "Maybe we should just take things a little slower." She stepped back, out of his reach, then smoothed her hands over her skirt. "I should go. I promised my mother I'd help her do some baking for Emma's party."

"I guess I'll see you tonight, then," Jake said.

Caley nodded. "Yeah. We'll see each other."

Jake wasn't about to let her go without just one more kiss. He grabbed her hand again and pulled her against his body. Kissing her had always been a wonderful prelude to other activities, but this time, Jake made sure that the kiss was enough to convey his feelings. He lingered over her mouth, softly drawing his tongue over her lower lip. When he finished, he walked outside with her and watched as she hiked back up to her car.

A few moments later, as if on cue, Sam reappeared from around the corner of the summer kitchen. He stared off in the direction of Caley and when she turned to wave, Sam waved back. "She looks good," he said.

"She does," Jake agreed.

"I'm glad she accepted my invitation to Emma's party."

Jake frowned. "You invited her?"

"Yeah. I saw her when I was in New York for that law school interview. I told her you missed her and that you couldn't live without her. I guess it worked, huh?"

A curse slipped from Jake's lips. "Why the hell did you tell her that?"

"Because it's the truth," Sam said, shaking his head. "Stop pretending you don't want each other." He chuckled. "Emma and I should lock you up and take away your clothes and shoes. Maybe you'd figure out you belong together."

"Taking away our clothes would not help the problem," Jake muttered. "We do really well without our clothes. It's when we're fully dressed that we can't figure things out." Jake grabbed the rope from Sam's hands and started toward the lake. "And just stay out of my business, will you? I can handle this on my own."

"Hey, you helped me and Emma. I'm just returning the favor."

Jake hefted the coil of rope over his shoulder. He wasn't really angry with Sam. His brother's intentions were good and right now he needed all the help he could get. He had no idea how to make things work with Caley, but he was going to try.

And if he couldn't make things work by the time she left for New York, then he'd be forced to sell all his stuff and move there.

MUSIC DRIFTED through the warm summer night, mixing with the rhythmic lapping of the water against the sandy shore. Caley sat on the beach, staring out across the water at the lights from the homes on the east shore. She tried to find a light from Havenwoods, wondering exactly where the house sat on the shoreline.

She hadn't visited the lake in the summer months since that summer before college and she'd forgotten how calm and peaceful it was at night. In the distance, a motorboat crawled across the water and the sound sent a pair of ducks into flight, their wings fluttering as they skimmed along the surface of the lake.

She used to believe New York City was the most wonderful place in the world to live. But after coming back to North Lake, she'd learned to appreciate its charms. It was quiet and pretty, a world away from the hustle and bustle of the city. And Jake was here, at least for a few days a week.

They'd circled around each other all night, chatting every now and then, before wandering away to talk to other party guests. Caley was grateful for the time and the buffer that her family provided. Though she'd been sorely tempted to jump back into bed with Jake, there were reasons not to.

"I thought I'd find you down here."

Caley jumped, startled by the sound of his voice. A moment later, Jake plopped down beside her on the sand, kicking off his sandals and setting them beside him. "I like this place a lot more in the summer," he said.

Caley took a deep breath, then slowly let it out. Her heart pounded in her chest and her throat had gone dry. She'd come all this way to tell him and now was the perfect time. "Jake, I need to say something."

"So do I," he said. "I've been wanting to—"

"No," Caley interrupted. "Me first. When I made my offer that evening of my eighteenth birthday, I thought I was grown-up enough to accept the consequences. You were right to refuse me. I've been hurt and angry with you ever since but for no good reason." She drew in another deep breath. "I'm going to make you another offer and this time, I promise I won't be angry if you refuse."

"You know what's really great about summer?" Jake asked.

Caley turned to look at him. Didn't he want to hear what she had to say? "Jake, I'm trying to—"

"Swimming. The water's pretty warm already. Especially on the other side of the lake at Havenwoods. You see, the wind usually blows from the west and it blows all the warm surface water over to that side. It's

probably five or ten degrees warmer on the east shore."
He stood up beside her and began to unbutton his
shirt. "I don't think it's too cold for skinny-dipping,
though."

Caley gasped as Jake continued to strip off his
clothes. His body was gorgeous in the moonlight, all
hard muscle and lean limbs. A tiny shiver skittered
down her spine and her fingers clenched with the
need to reach out and touch him.

When he was completely naked, he stood next to
her and waited. "Skinny-dipping doesn't work with
clothes on," he said.

"I'm not jumping in that water," Caley said.

"Come on. We can talk while we swim."

She shook her head, laughing at his audacious
request. "No. I'll freeze."

A moment later, Jake ran in, executing a perfect
shallow dive, his body slicing into the water with
barely a sound. He surfaced ten feet from the shore,
standing on his tiptoes on the bottom. "Come on,
Caley. I'll keep you warm."

"There are guests still up at the house. What if
they walk down here?"

"We can hide under the pier," he said.

"It sounds like you've done this before."

Jake laughed, then swam up to the pier. "No. But
I used to think about it all the time. It was the stuff
of my teenage fantasies. I used to think about you

and me, doing this. Taking off all our clothes and playing around in the water. And then, we'd just swim together and I'd be able to touch you. I loved that fantasy. I still do." He dunked his head under the water, then slicked his hair back. "Come on, Caley. You can say everything you want to say once we're in the water."

"You're crazy," she said.

"I'm in love with this smart, sexy woman," Jake countered. "I'm supposed to be crazy. What about you?"

Caley smiled, then shook her head. "Is it really cold?"

"No." He paused. "Well, maybe a little. But if you keep moving it's not bad. Come on, Caley Lambert. You used to rise to any challenge, accept any dare. You're turning into a wimp."

She got to her feet, staring out as he bobbed in the water. Then, Caley reached for the hem of her shirt and tugged it over her head. She kicked off her sandals and then skimmed her skirt down over her hips. When she stood in her underwear, Jake swam backward. But instead of running into the water, she walked slowly across the beach.

"It's not skinny-dipping unless you take everything off."

Groaning softly, she reached back and unhooked her bra, letting it fall off her shoulders. "Satisfied?"

"Not quite."

Grudgingly, Caley slid her panties down and kicked them aside. Then, holding her breath, she stepped in. She wasn't prepared for the temperature of the water. It wasn't cold, it was frigid, stealing her breath from her chest. When the water reached her knees, she pushed forward, submerging for a second before she surfaced, gasping and sputtering.

A moment later, his hands were on her body, holding on to her waist and pulling her farther from the shore until she could just barely touch the bottom. "Oh my God. A few degrees colder and we could play hockey."

They bobbed around for a while and to Caley's surprise, she did adjust. Before long, the air seemed colder than the water.

"See, it's not so bad," Jake said. She wrapped her arms around his neck and Jake slid his hands over her hips to cup her backside. "This is much better. Now, tell me what you wanted to say."

"Why did I have to come in the water to do that?"

"Because you can't tell me that you never want to see me again while we're swimming around naked together."

Caley kicked away from him, then splashed water in his face. "I want to see you," she said. "I don't want to be apart anymore." She shivered, her teeth chattering. "I quit my job. And sublet my apartment.

In a few days, I'm not going to have anywhere to live. I was thinking, maybe you might need a roommate at Havenwoods. I could help you out with the renovation."

"Are we talking about forever here?"

"Yes. I think that might be nice."

"I could do forever," Jake said.

"Really?" Caley asked. "You're sure?"

"I haven't been happy since you left. And I was getting ready to move to New York."

"Don't do that." She stared up at the stars. "This is where we belong."

Jake pulled her body against his, wrapping her legs around his waist and rubbing her back. "So, I guess we're going to be together," he murmured, brushing his lips against hers.

"We are," Caley said. Raking her fingers through his hair, she pulled him into a long, deep kiss, their warm mouths meeting and melding.

Suddenly, she wasn't afraid anymore. Loving Jake was the most natural thing in the world. It always had been from the time she'd first really seen him as the boy of her dreams. Whether it was fate or circumstance or just good luck, she'd found a man whom she could love. He'd been standing in front of her for so long that all she'd had to do was reach out and touch him.

"How much longer do we have to stay in this water?" she asked, her teeth still chattering.

"We could make a run for the boathouse. No one would find us there."

Caley thought about the warm blankets and the soft bed in the boathouse, then nodded. She wanted to crawl beneath the covers with Jake and to let him warm her body and arouse her desire. "I suppose it would be all right if someone did find us. We're going to have to tell our families sometime, don't you think?"

"Maybe we should do what Sam and Emma did. Just get married."

Caley kissed him again. "If we tell our mothers, you know they're going to want to plan a big wedding. They missed out with Sam and Emma. They're not going to take this well."

"I could always fly back to New York with you. We could get married there, spend our honeymoon in some fancy hotel and rent a truck and move your things back."

She smiled. "I like that idea."

This was the beginning of their life together, here where it nearly ended eleven years ago. It was better this way, Caley mused. It was meant to be this way. And years from now, when they stood on this same shore and looked out over the water, they'd remember the night of her eighteenth birthday. But they'd also remember the night they went skinny-dipping and decided that they might love each other forever.

Silhouette® Desire

NEW YORK TIMES BESTSELLING AUTHOR

DIANA PALMER

A brand-new Long, Tall Texans novel

IRON COWBOY

*Available March 2008
wherever you buy books.*

$1.00 OFF

The bestselling Lakeshore Chronicles continue with *Snowfall at Willow Lake*, a story of what comes after a woman survives an unspeakable horror and finds her way home, to healing and redemption and a new chance at happiness.

SUSAN WIGGS

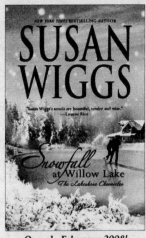

On sale February 2008!

SAVE $1.00 off the purchase price of **SNOWFALL AT WILLOW LAKE** by Susan Wiggs.

Offer valid from February 1, 2008, to April 30, 2008.
Redeemable at participating retail outlets. Limit one coupon per purchase.

52608168

Canadian Retailers: Harlequin Enterprises Limited will pay the face value of this coupon plus 10.25¢ if submitted by customer for this product only. Any other use constitutes fraud. Coupon is nonassignable. Void if taxed, prohibited or restricted by law. Consumer must pay any government taxes. Void if copied. Nielsen Clearing House ("NCH") customers submit coupons and proof of sales to Harlequin Enterprises Limited, P.O. Box 3000, Saint John, N.B. E2L 4L3, Canada. Non-NCH retailer—for reimbursement submit coupons and proof of sales directly to Harlequin Enterprises Limited, Retail Marketing Department, 225 Duncan Mill Rd., Don Mills, Ontario M3B 3K9, Canada.

65373 00076 2 (8100) 0 11463

U.S. Retailers: Harlequin Enterprises Limited will pay the face value of this coupon plus 8¢ if submitted by customer for this product only. Any other use constitutes fraud. Coupon is nonassignable. Void if taxed, prohibited or restricted by law. Consumer must pay any government taxes. Void if copied. For reimbursement submit coupons and proof of sales directly to Harlequin Enterprises Limited, P.O. Box 880478, El Paso, TX 88588-0478, U.S.A. Cash value 1/100 cents.

® and TM are trademarks owned and used by the trademark owner and/or its licensee.
© 2008 Harlequin Enterprises Limited

MSW2493CPN

Private jets. Luxury cars. Exclusive five-star hotels.
Designer outfits for every occasion and an entourage
to see to your every whim…

In this brand-new collection,
ordinary women step into the
world of the super-rich and are

TAKEN BY
THE MILLIONAIRE

Don't miss the glamorous collection:

MISTRESS TO THE TYCOON
by **NICOLA MARSH**

AT THE BILLIONAIRE'S BIDDING
by **TRISH WYLIE**

THE MILLIONAIRE'S
BLACKMAIL BARGAIN
by **HEIDI RICE**

HIRED FOR THE BOSS'S BED
by **ROBYN GRADY**

Available March 11
wherever books are sold.

nocturne™

Dark, sensual and fierce.
Welcome to the world of the
Bloodrunners, a band of hunters
and protectors, half human,
half Lycan. Caught between two
worlds—yet belonging to neither.

Look for the new miniseries by

RHYANNON
BYRD

LAST WOLF STANDING
(March 2008)

LAST WOLF HUNTING
(April 2008)

LAST WOLF WATCHING
(May 2008)

Available wherever books are sold.

www.silhouettenocturne.com

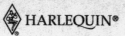

HARLEQUIN®

Blaze™

COMING NEXT MONTH

#381 GETTING LUCKY Joanne Rock
Blush

Sports agent Dex Brantley used to be the luckiest man alive. But since rumors of a family curse floated to the surface, he's been on a losing streak. To reverse that, he hooks up again with sexy psychic Lara Wyland. Before long he's lucky in a whole new way!

#382 SHAKEN AND STIRRED Kathleen O'Reilly
Those Sexy O'Sullivans, Bk. 1

When Gabe O'Sullivan describes his friend Tessa Hart as a work in progress, it gets Tessa to thinking. She's carried a torch for Gabe forever, but maybe now's the time to light the first spark and show him who's really ready to take their sexy flirting to the next level!

#383 OFF LIMITS Jordan Summers

Love happens when you least expect it. Especially on an airplane between Delaney Carter, an undercover ATF agent, and Jack Gordon, a former arms dealer. With their lives on the line, can they find a way to trust each other... once they're out of bed?

#384 BEYOND HIS CONTROL Stephanie Tyler

A reunion rescue mission turns life-threatening just as navy SEAL Justin Brandt realizes he's saving former high school flame Ava Turkowski. Talk about a blast from the past...

#385 WHAT HAPPENED IN VEGAS... Wendy Etherington

For Jacinda Barrett, leaving Las Vegas meant leaving behind her exotic dancer self. Now she's respectable...in every way. Then Gideon Nash—her weekend-she'll-never-forget hottie—shows up. Suddenly she's got the urge to lose the clothes...and the respectability!

#386 COMING SOON Jo Leigh
Do Not Disturb

Concierge Mia Traverse discovers a body in the romantic Hush hotel, which is booked for a movie shoot. Detective Bax Milligan is assigned to investigate and keep Mia under wraps. Hiding out with her in a sexy suite is perfect—except for *who* and *what* is coming next....

HBCNM0208